Be

The Journey of Rol

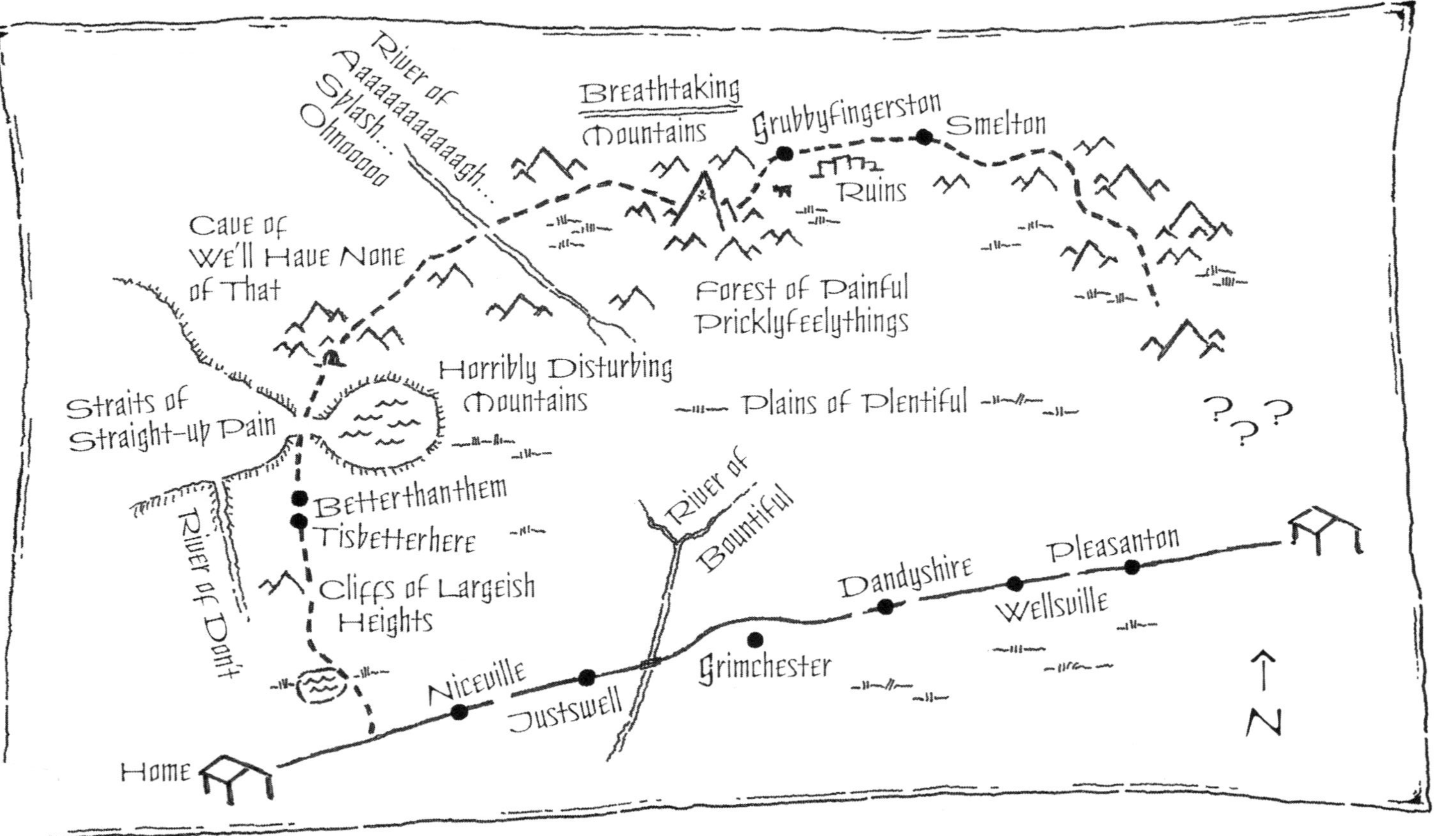
River of
Aaaaaaaaaaaaagh...
Splash...
Ohnooooo
Breathtaking
Mountains
Grubbyfingerston
Smelton
Ruins
Cave of
We'll Have None
of That
Forest of Painful
Pricklyfeelythings
Horribly Disturbing
Mountains
Straits of
Straight-up Pain
Plains of Plentiful
???
Betterthanthem
Tisbetterhere
River of
Bountiful
River of Don't
Cliffs of Largeish
Heights
Pleasanton
Dandyshire
Wellsville
Grimchester
Niceville
Justswell
Home
N

Be

The Journey of Rol

Ric Colegrove

Gabriel Creative Press

Published by Gabriel Creative Press - Warrenton, VA, USA.

ISBN: 978-0-9862643-0-6
Library of Congress Control Number: 2014921266

For information visit
www.thejourneyofrol.com

Book, cover design, and illustrations by Ric Colegrove

First printing, November 2014

To Betty, Lauren, and Andrew
who fill me with inspiration and joy
each and every day.

CHAPTER 1

SERIOUS BUFFOONERY

"Do you want the good news or the bad news first?"

It was a mind game that fourteen-year-old Rol often played with his much older uncle, Master DaTerrin.

"I'll take the bad news first, young impetuous one," replied DaTerrin. "And I do hope that this time the bad news is not as bad as it has been recently."

"Well, as you can see," started Rol innocently, "I don't have the items for the week that you sent me to get at the market." Rol held out his arms to show they were free of the expected edibles. "But instead"—and he paused for a moment and a half for effect—"I have these three tiny, speckled duck eggs." He held them forth in the palm of his right hand to be gazed upon in all their tiny, speckled duck egg glory.

The aged face of DaTerrin showed the glimmer of a

smile. His wrinkled lips trembled and then quivered, but he fought to control his reaction to the sight of the eggs in his nephew's palm. To make a further attempt at presenting a serious appearance, DaTerrin pinched his right eye whiskers between his thumb and forefinger, twirling them deliberately as he listened. He also furrowed his brow for good measure.

"And the good news," continued Rol, "is that they are magic eggs that, when eaten, will imbue whoever eats them with amazing powers like invisibility and incredible strength!" After another pause for effect, he added, "Before you doubt even the slightest bit, I'll have you know it's true. It is. I heard it from the merchant who sold them to me in town. He had to remind me what *imbue* meant, though."

A moment for the words to sink in.

Another. And one more.

Then, without warning, DaTerrin lost the smile battle and went straight into a laugh that quickly became hearty, on the brink of boisterous or even clamorous. It took some time for the elder to regain control. He had been semi-expecting a humorous remark from his nephew—based on past experience, especially recently—but not the one he had just heard. When the laughter subsided, after a few subsequent chuckle eruptions that came out of nowhere, he calmly said in a deadpan manner, "Magic duck eggs. That's a good one. Your wit knows no bounds. But tell me, my young jester, where are the supplies? The truth this time."

Rol shrugged playfully, but upon seeing his uncle's expression transition from that-was-quite-humorous-and-thank-you-for-the-good-laugh to I've-had-enough-for-the-moment-and-the-time-for-your-antics-is-over, he decided to end the high jinks.

"I'll be right back," Rol said, and ran hurriedly down the path toward the town he had visited earlier that morning. Standing a few steps in front of the door to his house, DaTerrin watched as his nephew stopped at the nearest tree, reached behind the large, gnarled trunk to grab something on the ground, and then stood up, placing his left hand on his hip while scratching the top of his head with his right. Rol hesitated for a moment and then slowly crouched. There were a few moments of shuffling and of gathering items in his arms, and then he came jogging back to DaTerrin, who waited for him, stone-faced.

"Do you want the good news or the bad news first?" asked Rol again, this time with a nervous crack in his voice.

"I would like them both," DaTerrin said, sounding frustrated. "The order doesn't matter, and this game must come to an end. Preferably a *satisfactory* end."

"The good news is that I went to the market and brought back everything—*everything*, mind you—that you asked me to get. The bad news is that I put all the items behind that tree"—Rol pointed, indicating the exact tree—"so that I could tell you about the duck eggs. And it appears that while we were talking, a few local skrats happened to get into the bread. Now we have one less loaf of bread for the week." Rol lowered his head, looking as sorry as he could in hopes of appearing properly distraught about the situation.

Rubbing his wispy white-and-gray beard thoughtfully with one ancient hand, DaTerrin contemplated the most appropriate reply that would reprimand his nephew without discouraging him. Rol knew perfectly well what was happening and stood motionlessly in front of his older and wiser uncle. He waited patiently for the elder's response, waited a little longer, and then—when it seemed he could not possibly wait another moment—he forced himself to wait longer still. Rol did so without uttering a sound and without any unnecessary fidgeting, such as scratching itchy spots or cracking his dirt-encrusted finger or toe knuckles. Rol was a good student and learned his lessons quickly. He also understood that although he had provoked a good laugh, it had been at the expense of a few days' worth of bread, which was costly and inconvenient to replace.

As he waited, Rol thought that the worst-possible reply from DaTerrin would be his uncle asking what *he* thought should be done. That's how it always happened. Master put

Rol on the spot, and that made Rol wish he had a carefully constructed answer—or even an array of appropriate comebacks—instead of some blubbering words and nonsensical phrases that didn't help the situation in any way, but instead often prolonged the agony.

"What do you think I should do about this?" the master asked wistfully.

I sure didn't see that coming, thought Rol sarcastically. He devised his comeback quickly. "Since you are asking, I think you should tell me what you would do so that I will gain knowledge from your great wisdom," replied the ever-sly student.

"I *will* tell you," said the even slyer teacher, "and then you will grace me with feedback to what I have said. But first, in all humility, as I am a student as well as a teacher, some words of wisdom: For those you first meet—as well as those you have known for ages—believe in them, have faith in them, give them your complete trust. If they would like you to feel or act otherwise, that is up to them."

DaTerrin let that sink in for a moment. Then another. And then one more moment to wrap it up in a neat little package.

While absorbing the wisdom that had been expressed so eloquently and collecting his admittedly inadequate thoughts, Rol chose his words carefully. Purposefully looking seriously serious, he replied, "You trusted me to bring back the items from the market. I was careless and let them out of my sight for the sake of a joke. I let you down and deserve some sort of punishment for betraying your trust and making you feel otherwise, just as you now mentioned in your words of unbelievably wise wisdom moment."

DaTerrin wrestled back a grin. Almost. "Yes, you were careless. But you were also quite humorous with your remark about magic. Not that funny makes up for careless, mind you. Yet, I do know that your heart was in the right place . . . even though your bag of food was not." The smile at last broke through fully, putting Rol at ease. "Let's consider this a lesson learned and a good deed done for those pesky skrats. Anyway, I can't wait to try those 'magic' duck eggs. The extra strength I don't need, but I've always wanted to know what it would be like to suddenly disappear."

Back in his room, after helping his uncle put away the items from the market, Rol looked out a cobweb-laden window at a brief rain shower and reflected on the encounter with his uncle. He was amused by how similar it had been to many of their interesting interactions. Moments of fun, periods of seriousness, a reasonable ending that led Rol to later reflect on the experience. Most likely it all unfolded in exactly the way his uncle had planned, which did not both-

er Rol a bit. The time with DaTerrin was often predictably unpredictable as much as it was organized chaos, but Rol believed he benefited from all the training and experiences. His master sometimes referenced their sessions as "serious buffoonery," which described the various situations well.

Although Rol's uncle was much, much older—or "wiser," as DaTerrin preferred to think of the gap—and therefore had much more life experience than he did, secretly, Rol longed for the knowledge and enlightenment his uncle had earned and now displayed. They shared a common bond when it came to the quest for knowledge.

In terms of appearance, though, the two were wildly different. Rol was thin and tall for his age, while his uncle was pudgy and not so tall, a difference that Rol referred to at times by calling his uncle "Little Master"—but only when he thought he could get away with it. The boy had bright green eyes and mostly smooth skin, as opposed to the elder, who had mysterious gray eyes and weathered but not unduly wrinkled, pale skin. Rol's hair was dark brown and curly, but DaTerrin had little hair on his head—and most of the hair he did have appeared to have migrated down to his small chin, from which a long, whitish-gray beard sprouted. More wispy hair poked out playfully from DaTerrin's bumpy nose and knotted ears.

Both Rol and his uncle had generally cheerful outlooks

and good manners—though when it came to eating without slurping, neither would be counted among the civilized. Both had surprisingly quick reflexes, and both enjoyed challenges, puzzles, and deciphering as well as witty banter, if they did say so themselves. The two discovered they both also appreciated music. DaTerrin whistled joyfully when he awoke at sunrise each day, and Rol lay in bed in the next room, listening to the playfully shrill sound before committing to the day by putting his sockless feet on the rugless floor.

DaTerrin's voice interrupted the daydreaming Rol.

"If you are not too preoccupied, young one," said Rol's uncle, "would you consider walking with me to the market to replace that bread?"

A brief return to the village market quickly became much more exciting than the shopping trip just that morning, even with its speckled duck eggs prank.

Upon arriving in the market area, Rol heard shouts of "Thief! Stop!" from a nearby shop. He and DaTerrin turned to see a black-robed man running out of the shop with a pouch in one hand and a small stick in the other. The shop owner chased after the man but stopped abruptly at the entrance. Others in the area gathered around to help, but they backed away swiftly as the man raised the stick and pointed threateningly at each bystander, then sweeping the air with it to hold them all at bay.

"Mind you, I have a wand of foul spells," cried the robed man, who pulled back the hood of his cloak to get a better view. Rol noted that his hair was white, and his eyes were wild and black. The man continued in a booming and obnoxious voice, "I am Darkor, son of Darklor. Do not test me, or you will pay dearly." He confidently wielded the stick, which was presumably the wand he had mentioned earlier, and continued to point it menacingly at the frightened townsfolk. He also started backing his way toward the main path in and out of the village.

DaTerrin moved toward Rol and whispered a few words in his ear. Rol replied with a strange look and the words: "Are you sure?"

DaTerrin nodded and moved away quickly, around the outer edge of the crowd and toward the man known—at least to himself—as Darkor. Rol watched his uncle and then tentatively stepped into an open area that had been vacated by bystanders, putting himself between them and the self-acclaimed son of Darklor.

"Excuse me," muttered Rol. The white-haired man stopped. He tilted his head slightly as he tried to make sense of the situation. A younger was addressing him. There was no movement from anyone in the crowd, at least that he could see. And nothing threatening about the boy, but something was not right.

Suddenly, the man in black felt a tug on the back of his hood. When he wheeled around, he came chest to face with a man who seemed to be about his age but who was smaller and with more nose and ear hair. Pointing his wand at the whiskered newcomer, Darkor said, again in that obnoxious voice, "I am Darkor, son of Darklor. Who dares confront me and the wrath of my powerful wand?" And then he pointed his highfalutin stick in DaTerrin's face.

DaTerrin smiled pleasantly at the man. He made a quick motion to the left, then back to the right, and then he raised both hands and put his thumbs in his ears while wiggling his fingers at Darkor. The wand followed DaTerrin's movements, but no further action was taken.

DaTerrin taunted the irritating man for a few more moments, practically inviting him to demonstrate his wizardry. When Darkor did nothing, DaTerrin snatched the wand from him, spun it around twice in his fingers, and rapped one end on the fleshy tip of his opponent's pointy nose. In a complete stupor, the dazed man in black watched DaTerrin snap the wand in two while sweeping his right foot behind Darkor's ankles. DaTerrin then pushed Darkor in the chest, a move that immediately caused him to drop to the ground, bringing embarrassment to Darkor, as well as papa Darklor, whoever he was. Flat on his back, and with an absolutely stunned expression, the would-be thief and self-proclaimed wizard lay helpless and silent while some of the menfolk from the village swaggered in to hold him down.

Rol rushed to his uncle and hugged him tightly. "I know I should have been confident, but I was too scared," he said, apologetically. "I thought he would turn you into a larch bird or some such creature."

"He did," quipped DaTerrin with a wink, "But I recovered quickly."

A few bystanders, who happened to be bystanding around and were obviously eavesdropping, laughed and patted DaTerrin and Rol on their backs, and then continued with their business of being background extras. As the crowd dispersed and Darkor was taken away in chains, Rol asked his mentor how he had known the man would not use his wand to cast a spell on him.

"I've lived a long, long time, young one," his uncle said. "I've seen many interesting and inexplicable things. But I've never seen a magic object live up to its reputation. The truth is, magic wands *aren't*. Transforming spells *don't*. Scrolls and potions are just fancy names for paper and liquid. Darkor knew his wand was useless. I could see it in his eyes. He was more afraid than you, although he covered his fear well with his deep, confident voice."

"But . . ."

"Why are there so many stories of magical happenings? People are bored, so they make up tales of wizards and sorcery. Or they try to take advantage of someone who will believe them, as Mr. *Dorkor* tried to do a few moments ago. The best way to handle that situation is to confront the person. Call him out. And if you can show others the lie at the same time—well, all the better."

Rol said that he thought he understood. Then, after settling down from the excitement, as he and his uncle continued their market day rounds, he joked, "I *wand*er what will happen to the man in black."

"He'll be sitting a *spell* in prison, I'm sure," wisecracked DaTerrin.

They both agreed that the punnery should end there.

CHAPTER 2

STICKS AND STONES

Back in DaTerrin's cottage, Rol and his uncle sat by a warm fire and laughed about their encounter with the faux wizard. Despite their agreement, their puns continued through the night, although they will not be discussed further here. It did give master and student time to reflect on important lessons—some that were scheduled, and some that were not, as with the day's Darkor encounter.

Rol mentioned that he wished he had brought his Stick to the market, and how he would have given the man in black a lesson he would not soon forget.

Rol's favorite activity was sparring with Battlesticks—or Sticks, as they called them. They were basically walking sticks, with a more intimidating name and more gashes, but they were effective weapons. Rol was a quick learner.

He thought swiftly and reacted quickly in mock battles, his body moving without hesitation. Unfortunately for Rol, all his battle encounters had been nothing more than planned learning experiences with DaTerrin. As it turned out, he had no enemies, and the land he inhabited with his uncle was generally at peace, other than his having to put up with the occasional bully.

Rol expressed that he longed for more challenging experiences in battle, but DaTerrin stressed that one should never go looking for a fight. He reminded his nephew that the reason to train was not to instigate but to defend—whether it was he or others he hoped to protect. There were times, DaTerrin explained, when the decision whether to put oneself in certain dangerous situations had to be made, and that determination hinged on many factors. Rol understood but still wanted to be tested in a real, life-threatening encounter.

"I'm sure that opportunity will come soon enough, young one," his teacher said.

Rol asked DaTerrin why they should not use a sharp weapon such as a sword or battle-axe. Surely, he suggested, even a Battlestick with a blade attached would be more lethal.

The answer from his uncle came swiftly and solemnly. "Used correctly, and for the right reason, these Sticks are lethal enough," DaTerrin said. "Pray that you will never find that out for yourself. Always remember that if you are attacked, seek not to kill but only to disarm or render the other, or others, unable to continue. Taking someone's life is a serious matter. It is something that never leaves you, and we will not discuss it any further at this time."

DaTerrin walked away to be by himself, leaving Rol to wonder why the air had suddenly become so cold, even by the fire. After a few moments, attempting to reverse the abrupt change in mood, Rol picked up a small twig lying by the fireplace and darted after his master, good-humoredly shouting taunts while swinging wildly.

That night, in the silence of his own room, Rol's thoughts were on his father, and how he would have handled that day's situation.

At Rol's age, his father was taken to a supposedly wiser man to train as a stonewright's apprentice. In addition to learning the physically demanding trade, his father engaged in training that involved strenuous hand-to-hand combat. Stories of his training had mesmerized Rol and other youngers at family gatherings. The presumably tall tales told of his father wrestling wild boars using only the strength in his abnormally huge forearms and taking down giants with a sweep of his thick hands.

Apparently, the plan for Rol's training was similar,

although focused as much on life experiences as on physical training. *I'm an apprentice but not a manservant,* thought Rol as he considered the chores he was often asked to do. He would never be comfortable spending his days at the beck and call of another, although, truthfully, he had never spent much time at *anyone's* beck and call, whatever a beck was anyway. Following more or less in his dear father's foot- . . . or rather, *boot* steps, he was taken to DaTerrin's humble abode to study and master the craft he was meant to master. And according to the plan, he would return to his parents when he was a few years older and wiser to "practice" his craft at home. (*Practice* was an odd word choice in that, theoretically, he would already be a master—which by definition meant he would not *need* practice.) Then he would continue with a happy life, such as his father's appeared to be. That was that.

But that was *not* that.

It was nothing like that. *This* was much more than *that.*

CHAPTER 3

"WHEN YOU ARE READY"

Three years prior, after what seemed an eternity of miserable travel with his parents by way of a large two-horse wagon, Rol had arrived at his uncle's small cottage in a dangerously feverish state. He was ill for several days, and his mother and father spoke in hushed tones about whether he would survive. Specific details were foggy, but Rol remembered fragments of comments his parents had made. They sounded uneasy about leaving him for so long—especially when he was suffering from a serious illness of unknown origin. His uncle's words had apparently reassured Rol's parents. DaTerrin explained that the plans the three of them had made were necessary for the greater good. Even so, Rol's mother was distraught at the prospect of leaving her only son behind.

Rol also vaguely remembered the day, not long after he arrived at his uncle's, that his parents actually left him. He was not able to properly express his feelings at a moment that could have proved to be the last time they would see each other.

Feeling painfully alone the first few weeks, Rol regularly questioned why he had been left at his uncle's, without close family around him, not counting his uncle of course. It was very difficult to be him, and he was sure that no one else could understand his feelings. His parents had previously explained that he needed "special" training, adding that neither they nor anyone else in their village could provide it. Apparently, the task of raising Rol on a temporary basis fell to the brother of his mother, Uncle A. Loysius DaTerrin, for which *temporary* was never clearly defined. Rol couldn't grasp the arrangement, and he complained about it constantly during the first few weeks of his stay.

In those early days with his mysteriously inexplicable and altogether enigmatic uncle, Rol discovered that he and DaTerrin were a good combination as teacher and student, and both enjoyed the relationship. Apparently, they had met once many years prior, although Rol was young at the time and didn't remember the encounter.

"What should I call you?" asked Rol three days after his parents left. "Uncle, teacher, mentor, DaTerrin, A. Loysius?"

"You are free to call me what you wish, and I would add *friend* to the list," his uncle replied. "But uncle, teacher, and master seem most appropriate—thank you for asking."

"Is *master* the correct term? That doesn't make me a slave or servant, does it? I definitely would not like that."

"No, of course not, young one. It only refers to me as one who is accomplished and experienced, and helps define your role as an apprentice. Use the term or not, as you wish. It is respectful to me without meaning to demean you in any way. In prior times—and this was a long time ago, mind you—others have called me master. At first it was difficult for me to accept, in all humility. But with the knowledge that I have attained, I realize that it seems appropriate, without setting me above others. I am no better than any other. I just happen to have lived longer than anyone else . . . even the mountains." At this DaTerrin smiled. Rol chuckled and decided that he would try each name on occasion, to see which fit the best, before deciding on one or two to use. Or three. But no more than four.

The days went by, and Rol eventually felt comfortable in the new environment. It was different from what he was accustomed to, as just about everything else in his new life was, but it was also incredibly exciting. His uncle's house was solidly constructed and decorated uniquely with knick-knacks, doohickeys, and interesting collections of thingamabobs. It was also dry, and spacious enough for the two of them as well as any visitors who happened by, though they had few guests, except on Tax-Collector Tuesdays. The land around was fresh and green. The nearby town was smallish, but it was large enough—with its shops and vendors—to provide whatever they could not grow, build, or otherwise create themselves.

Over time Rol had come to realize he had no real reason to complain. His special training mostly meant using his creative and ever-inquisitive mind in ways that were beyond what most others his age were experiencing back home—*home* being the place he had lived with his mother, father, and two sisters, not this home, now, which was still sometimes confusing, even after three years. Rol didn't know for sure what others were being taught or how. But previously, as a younger in his village, he attended lessons with others his age, give or take a few years. Because there were many students, the attention was not as focused on him, which he preferred. Now it was always just one teacher and one student—DaTerrin and Rol—and lessons moved along as fast or as slow as needed to ensure that Rol would absorb them.

Rol missed his family and the comforts in that life at home, including his mother's wonderful cooking and his father's amazing tales of grand adventure. He even missed his sisters, who were often pesky but also mostly like friends. He especially missed his sisters' hugs, though he would never tell them that.

Looking back, Rol realized that those difficult early weeks with DaTerrin were a necessary, although frustrating and lonely, adjustment period. He and his uncle established a strong bond during that time, which had also forced Rol to dig deep for the strength he would need to face the challenges he imagined lay ahead.

A few days after the encounter with Darkor, on a sunny but crisp morning, Rol and DaTerrin walked down the manicured path behind the elder's cottage, through an orchard of glossy rainfruit. The large bluish-orange orbs were hanging precariously from the strong branches, waiting to be picked within a few sunsets before they fell to the ground of their own accord and broke open, releasing the fragrant and sticky juice treasured by kings and vermin alike. This almost-weekly ritual was not an exhaustive walk physically but one that often led to exhaustive teacher-student discussions about life.

"Master, why do we pray?" Rol asked after a few moments of contemplation. He was always in the role of the student when with DaTerrin, the teacher.

"Why do you *think* we pray?" DaTerrin quickly replied.

Of course, Rol knew that would be the reply. And he was prepared on this occasion with an appropriate response. At least *he* thought it appropriate. "To ask for something. To seek guidance. To request assistance when in danger or in a difficult situation."

"To ask. To seek. To request. Very interesting." His uncle nodded. "Those are benefits to you. Anything else?"

"To ask for good things to happen to you, too. Not just for me."

"Thank you for that. And anything else?"

"Hmm. I cannot think of anything else, Master."

"What about being thankful? Not just asking for something but also to say that you appreciate what you have been given?"

"I never thought of that."

"Now you will."

That was a typical conversation between DaTerrin and Rol. A starting question, an ending statement. Both were appropriate, both were significant; one was often wiser and larger in scope than the other. The aged DaTerrin was a master of simplicity who taught wisdom, not just facts to memorize. He appeared to know everything, even when he asked his student "What are you thinking?" at a particular moment, which he did often.

In answering the "What are you thinking?" question,

Rol would often wittily reply that he was pondering his life as one amid the multitude of humble creatures in the vast world. Sometimes he would say instead that he was considering foreverness and how it might affect the current weather conditions in their land. But the master generally surmised that the real answer was that the apprentice was at least somewhat hungry and thinking about his next meal, which was often dead-on. And this day was no different—in part because they had skipped their typical morning meal but mostly because the rainfruit aroma was overwhelming their senses and causing their insides to rumble in response.

"It is fine. Take a fruit," DaTerrin said. "They must be picked soon anyway, and that one looks ready to leap."

Amazingly, as Rol cupped his hands under the aromatic sphere, it shuddered slightly and then dropped into his hands, as if on command. Producing a knife from his shoulder sheath, he split the fruit into two halves. Carefully, without spilling the brightly colored juice, he carved one half into a bowl. The other half was sectioned into bite-size pieces. Holding the bottom of the rainfruit bowl, he offered slices to DaTerrin, who gratefully chose two and dipped them into the juice for an additional treat.

Eating a rainfruit was a blessing in life, but you had to be quick about it. Once the fruit was opened, the air somehow immediately drew the flavor from it. Which is to say that if the fruit wasn't devoured quickly, it became dull taste-wise. Not wanting to miss the delicious moment, Rol grabbed three slices himself. And so the teacher and student stood in the morning mist and smiled bright bluish-orange smiles while enjoying the hurried, but indescribably tasty meal.

As Rol was exposed to many new concepts and experiences, he became more dependent on his uncle while at the same time striving to become more independent. It was strange to feel the dual tugs. The feelings confused him, and so he asked his teacher what was ahead for the two of them. Rol wasn't necessarily ready to move on, but he wanted to understand whatever arrangements his parents had made with DaTerrin.

When asked, his uncle didn't hesitate to reply. "When you are ready, it will be a time of decision," he said. "I cannot make the choice for you, now or even then. It will be up to you. Your parents and I have discussed this, and we have come to an agreement. They love you deeply and want what is best for you, as do I. At the same time, you can help them in ways that you cannot yet imagine. All is, and will be, up to you."

"You have said so many puzzling things since I came here," Rol replied. "But that is one of the most cryptic nonanswers you have ever given. Next you will probably say, 'You will know when you are ready.' Right?"

"I was going to say it will happen in exactly three weeks, but now I am not sure if you will be ready then, based on what you just said, Mr. Smarty-Tunic."

CHAPTER 4

THE NIGHT

Rol woke to the feeling of something wet on his face. *Wet* as in a drip of rain; *wet* as in a face covered with premorning dew; *wet* as in a sweat that came from a dream he just had.

It was The Night. Master DaTerrin had tried to prepare Rol for it for the past three weeks, but there was no preparing for something of this nature. It was to be experienced and endured, and there was no real way to train for such a time, although all his training had led to this.

Rol was in the forest-jungle, alone. All alone. All night, so far, which could lead into more than one night. DaTerrin had said that depending on what happened during The Night, it might end up being The Nights. After the night he just had, which wasn't quite finished with him yet, Rol hoped that would not be so. It was still dark.

Was DaTerrin out there, in the bushes? Would he leave Rol completely alone all night? Surely he would not. But Rol did not hear any human sounds at all during the night. There were almost-deafening animal and insect and possibly plant noises at times, but no sounds—not even snoring—that he could identify as belonging to his master and trainer. DaTerrin typically fell asleep easily and quickly. Rol knew this from having spent each night for the past three years sleeping in his room not far from DaTerrin's. Rol's uncle also had a habit of snoring as loud as a summer thunderstorm whenever and however he slept—afternoon or evening, deep sleep or quick happy nap.

Rol was lost and had been running almost since the day had turned dark. Something large had chased him briefly, and then several small somethings, and then another large something, although it was impossible to tell if the latest large thing was the same as the first large thing. It did not matter much, as Rol had been on the verge of exhaustion for some time and now his head was spinning.

With the first large creature—or the first time the one large creature had chased him, whatever the case might have been—Rol had decided to run for a short time, planning to then turn to confront his unseen attacker. Rol was skilled at using his Battlestick and confident in his abilities. That was, until the large black shape took a powerful swipe at him, knocking his Stick away and sending Rol to the muddy ground.

Quickly, Rol rolled away and onto his feet. Looking at the advancing shape that was at least twice as tall as he, Rol then ran in the opposite direction to put as much distance between himself and the large thing so that he had some time to consider his options. He left the creature behind but too soon heard the smaller others from his left side, prompting him to continue his flight in a different direction. With less than a moment to catch his breath, he was pursued by another large creature until at last he found temporary but painful refuge in a patch of thorn bushes.

Was DaTerrin hiding somewhere close by, unseen and unheard in the dark night? If so, why didn't he help Rol? If not, why not?

And with that thought he exhausted the last remains of his mental energy, causing an instinctive need for his body to completely shut down so his brain wouldn't push it any longer.

Waking in an unsettled state after a brief doze, Rol tried to clear his head and consider his options. Run? Continue to hide? Yell for help?

Unfortunately, reflecting on his next step distracted Rol from his immediate environment.

He was aware of a leap, though he detected it too late.

A muscular and hairy lizard appeared out of the brush, pinning Rol to the ground before he could sneeze, which is usually what happened when he was anywhere near the hairy lizards that grew to the size of a large man, not including the tail. His was a rare allergy and especially untimely, given the circumstances.

The lizard was surprisingly light, though, and Rol easily pushed it to the side while rolling effortlessly up on his knees and then rising to his feet. Unfortunately, the creature had drooled on Rol, and the acidic saliva burned a hole through his tunic and into his left shoulder. Rol's heart sank as his shoulder throbbed.

"Never lose hope," DaTerrin had said before The Night, "or all will be lost."

"And don't lose your socks, either. Good socks are hard to come by."

Wincing from the pain, Rol assessed the damage and realized that his shoulder wouldn't be of much use anytime soon. The lizard walked away lazily, probably off to find weaker and less dexterous prey. Rol wanted to sound brave by saying something such as "'Tis but a flesh wound!" But he couldn't muster the courage to speak, what with the pain being so bad.

Hearing a rustle advancing in the thicket next to him, the unarmed and temporarily one-shouldered Rol braced every muscle in his body for another fierce attack. But the threat turned out to be only DaTerrin, too little too late. His master would have appreciated that joke, but it went unsaid as Rol collapsed in his teacher's arms.

Later that day, Rol awoke to the sound of DaTerrin clanging in the other room.

"Can't someone with a life-threatening wound get any sleep around here?" Rol inquired feebly.

"'Tis but a flesh wound," replied his uncle, entering Rol's room with a tray of various healing elixirs and comfort food. They both had a good laugh, although Rol wasn't sure whether laughter was a good idea at the time, given the pain it brought on.

Sitting by the flickering fire that night, uncle and nephew spoke about the previous evening's adventure. Rol was honest about being disappointed in himself. DaTerrin dismissed his comments, saying, "Don't ever feel let down by yourself. You had quite a night and you survived. It is not a time to wallow in sorrowful thoughts but to instead gather your strength for the next time you may need to rely on it."

"I understand, Master," replied Rol, and their conversation turned to the excitement Rol felt and the eventual outcome of the outing.

"I just wonder, Uncle, what you would have done if I had not survived," Rol added thoughtfully. Or what would have happened if it had been you facing the challenge, and in the end I was left alone."

DaTerrin hesitated a few moments before replying, "If you had not survived. Hmm . . . I do not want to think about that. If I had not survived, I would like to think that you would say a few nice words about me and then find your way back to your village, to where you belong—with your family."

Now it was time for Rol to have a few moments of contemplation. "But how would I get there?" he asked at last. "You have never mentioned how to find the way, other than saying it is near Mapina-something and that the trek there can be long and arduous."

"Mapinashu it is, and the trek to your home can be considerably more difficult than arduous. But let us not talk of that now—you rest. Talk of further adventures must wait until tomorrow."

The next day came and, instead of continuing their talk, DaTerrin said it was necessary for him to address some local matters with the elders. He added that while he was in town, Rol could tend to some light chores around the house if he felt up to it—basically, if his left shoulder was in the mood. After a few moments alone in the quiet house, Rol did feel mostly up to doing anything other than lying in bed doing nothing.

Rol was a fidgetarian, someone who typically feels the need to do something instead of doing nothing. Fidgetarianism was a deeply entrenched trait in his family, going back to ancient times when his grandmother's grandmother's grandmother had a grandmother whose grandmother constantly tapped her toes and elbows throughout the day. No music in the air, no rhythm, just tapping. Rol didn't see anything wrong with that, and he had also gotten used to his father tapping food on the table during most meals, which was particularly messy on soup nights. Rol was not an incessant tapper, but he did fidget, which meant that he generally liked to be busy. It also meant that he had great dexterity, which came in handy for juggling objects and rolling coins or small stones through his fingers.

So, while waiting for DaTerrin, Rol spent the day cleaning what he could, trying to one-handedly juggle what he found lying haphazardly on the floor, and making a meal while balancing on one leg, tapping his toes.

By the time his uncle returned, it was dark. They ate the dinner Rol had prepared, and DaTerrin complimented the younger on the tasty meal. Although Rol wanted to continue the previous night's discussion, their conversation led to other matters instead of the "further adventures." There were other distractions during the next few days, though at last a day arrived when teacher and student could resume their talk. By then Rol had many questions.

DaTerrin had few direct answers, but the conversation lasted all day and late into the night. DaTerrin spoke of many tales that he had heard and some adventures he had experienced when he was a younger. He had visited many strange lands, and in each he had learned something valuable from the inhabitants—or instead provided important words or deeds to them.

It wasn't until way past the time for them to turn in that Rol understood three of the most important lessons DaTerrin had learned in his travels:

Be thankful.

Be good.

Be who you are meant to be.

Those insights combined to make up an overall philosophy that DaTerrin felt was most important in life: Be.

"Be?" questioned the engaged but sleepy student.

"Yes, exactly," answered the teacher, without really answering anything.

"But I don't completely understand what you mean by 'Be,' and I'm hoping that you can explain further," said Rol, stifling a yawn.

"It is time for you to go to sleep, young Rol. But so that you are not up the rest of the night thinking, I will say only that I cannot fully explain at this time—and we will have to leave it at that," said DaTerrin.

Well, that doesn't help at all, thought Rol a few moments later in his bed, pulling a blanket up to his shoulders. "'I cannot fully explain at this time?' What does that mean?" But before he could think any further, the day's conversation caught up with him and he fell into a heavy sleep, dreaming of great adventures in which he played the lead role.

CHAPTER 5

THE OTHER NIGHT

It was bright and sunny when Rol awoke the next day, mainly because Rol slept in so late. Everyone else in the world had already made their beds, brushed their teeth, and milked whatever animals needed milking. DaTerrin had promised an eventful day in which they would continue a lesson from many days ago. It was the third and final part of that lesson and the one that Rol was most excited about.

Student and teacher took their usual morning walk through the orchards, but this time the promise of an exciting day—for both—kept their usual conversation to a minimum. They returned to the house and packed a hearty lunch, as DaTerrin had explained they had a long walk in front of them. Comfortable footwear on, carved walking sticks in hand, Rol carrying the food in a bag slung over his left shoulder, which had healed nicely, and they were off.

Along the way, DaTerrin mentioned that the day would be much different from The Night that Rol had experienced not long ago. This part of the lesson was about finding calm, and that started with prayer.

"That could be a thankful prayer, not just one asking for something, right, Uncle?" said Rol. DaTerrin smiled at the boy for demonstrating his understanding of a lesson they had previously discussed.

"Correct, young one. I'm glad to know that you have been listening."

The conversation continued as the two walked on a path that was sometimes well marked and at other times almost nonexistent. They traveled to the top of the nearest hill-mountain—a flat, grassy area with a panoramic view—and ate lunch. Then DaTerrin continued with the lesson that had begun a few days ago, making a mental note of the position of the sun since they did not bring any source of light or any materials with which to start a fire.

They crouched down and knelt on the grass, facing away from each other, at least a couple of arm's lengths apart and from any bushes or tall grass. DaTerrin said that their eyes were to be closed and they should try to shut out the world's noises around them—the wind in the trees, the tiny speckers in the grass, their own breathing sounds. Doing so was a challenge for Rol. All the more so because DaTerrin breathed like a full-grown hog, though slightly less growly, but it was doable with focus.

"What shall we pray for?" Rol asked after a brief period of time, breaking the non-serenity.

"We shall pray that you learn to keep quiet at times like this," breathe-growled DaTerrin, his eyes still closed.

A few moments of actual silence followed, and then the teacher said, "Since you are curious, young one, we are not going to pray *for* anything. This lesson is about relationship. Keep your eyes closed so that your surroundings don't distract you at this time. Realize that you are tiny in this large world, and even tinier still in the world beyond this world. God is immensely large and capable of very large deeds and ideas. You are small, God is large. You are but one being, sitting right here, and God is all around and everywhere, always. That's the proper relationship . . . and your proper place."

Rol remained on his knees, for what seemed to be an immeasurably long time, considering that relationship and his place in the world. He felt small. Very small.

"Now. Quickly. Open your eyes!" shouted DaTerrin unexpectedly.

Rol immediately opened his eyes and took in the magnificence of the world around him. The sun was breaking through the clouds, and from the top of the hill-mountain he could see what seemed to be an everlasting everything. Although he had felt small previously, he felt a different smallness now . . . but also a great happiness.

His uncle's voice was full of joy. "This is what we have been given. Be grateful. We did not create any of it. Be humble. Someone else created it specifically for us. Be happy and thankful. That is our prayer—a Thank-You."

As Rol absorbed it all, DaTerrin continued, "The One who is larger than you created this for you. For *you*. He can do anything and is always there for you. You may be small, but you have a large friend. And he's a good listener. He will help you be anything you want, if you just ask. Realize, Rol, that throughout your life, no matter what, you should never be afraid, and you should never feel alone."

The words "never be afraid" and "never feel alone" echoed in Rol's ears. It was an incredible lesson, and more than what Rol had expected or imagined.

Both master and student basked in the beauty of their surroundings. Rol wanted to stay there into the night, but DaTerrin said that they should start walking home. He explained that it would be dark soon and reminded Rol they did not have torches. Rol convinced him to stay a bit longer so they could see the bright sun turn red and then disappear into the darkening horizon. They did, and the sunset was one of the most awe-inspiring sights Rol had ever seen.

And then it was dark. Not quite *dark* dark, but getting there.

DaTerrin sounded concerned when he said, "We should have left sooner. Now we must hurry or we will lose our way."

They quickly gathered the remnants of the food they had enjoyed while watching the birds, trees, hills, and distant clouds. Grabbing their walking sticks, they started down the hill-mountain as DaTerrin looked for clues to remind him of the way they had come. It got darker as they moved farther from the peak—and darker still in areas where the trees blocked out the now blue-black sky. Rol did not say a word as he followed his uncle, seeking clues as to their whereabouts while silently berating himself for having delayed their departure.

Still, they seemed to be making good progress. Suddenly, they heard a noise in the distance that was not at all welcome in the darkness that engulfed them. Although they were armed with their Sticks, a wild animal sound—or multiple sounds—was not what they were hoping to hear. Far-fetched though the notion was, someone yodeling and shouting "Follow my voice and I shall lead you to safety! Come on!" would have been preferred, maybe even desired. Instead, the sound of several creatures grunting was getting closer, as was a glow that appeared to be made up of several small torches.

"Grumblegoblins," said DaTerrin, shivering noticeably.

Rol had heard of the tiny beasties in stories when he was very young. They were feared and despised, and although not seen frequently, they were the subject of many ancient tales and epic poems, as well as a recent play that attempted to present the unseen gentle side of the terribly horrible creatures. A line from act 3, scene 2 announced: "They are just misunderstood."

DaTerrin wanted to yell "Run!" but was unsure of the best direction to safety, and running in the darkness without a plan was a sure way to lose each other. Knowing that grumblegoblins were good climbers, the elder decided that hiding in a tree would not help in this situation. Their best option was to find a place where they could lie or crouch down in bushes that would maybe hide them while the group passed by. They did the best they could and, looking at each other's camouflage, agreed that it would be difficult for them to be detected if they stayed motionless and silent.

The band of goblin-things arrived sooner than expected. DaTerrin confirmed that they were indeed grumblegoblins, based on their size—approximately that of a large duck, assuming you could stand one of them next to a duck long enough to measure properly, which you definitely could not.

Grumblegoblins were not large by any means, but they were known to travel in groups of thirty-seven and were ferocious warriors, especially when food was involved. They were chubby, smelly, and covered in thick, matted hair, with long feet and hands that ended in sharp claws. Their jaundiced yellow eyes saw well in almost any lighting situation, but their most powerful sense was that of smell, which unfortunately was not mentioned in any poem or legend. Their teeth were scraggly and almost as yellow as their eyes, and they had black lips that were constantly swollen from rubbing on their unkempt teeth. The present horde was moving quickly, appearing to be on its way to somewhere important, which DaTerrin took as a positive sign that Rol's and his chances were improving.

Then one of the hideous creatures stopped, sniffing the air.

DaTerrin immediately noticed the bag of food remnants lying near him, open. He used his walking stick to try to quietly close it. Unfortunately, the sniffing monstrosity came closer. It let out a screech, seeing DaTerrin and smelling the food morsels at the exact same moment. All the others stopped and turned to face the master.

Moving in closer, they surrounded him but, surprisingly, did not notice Rol, who was far enough away that the food bits attracted their snot-filled noses instead. DaTerrin looked directly at Rol and shook his head slightly, attempting to silently signal Rol not to do anything rash.

Rol saw his uncle mouth the word "Be."

Immediately, the beasts were upon DaTerrin, overpowering him and wrapping his entire body with crudely made ropes, much as a spider wraps her prey. Ten of the little horrors laid their captive horizontally and hoisted him up on their shoulders while the others held the group's torches and other belongings. They swiftly carried the teacher through the underbrush and off into the night. DaTerrin suddenly disappeared, leaving Rol alone and defeated.

After the initial shock, Rol realized that he was responsible for his uncle's fate. Gathering his courage, Rol stood up and started to follow the grumblegoblins. Not knowing the area, he found that keeping pace with the group of unspeakable somethings in the dark was next to impossible, if not right on top of it.

Rol could see the faint light of their torches, but it was growing dimmer by the moment. The beasts were extremely fast on their tiny but muscular legs, and soon he was unable to see their light at all. Rol stumbled on through the night, his tear-stained cheeks slapped by unseen tree branches.

It wasn't long before Rol completely lost his way, but he continued the chase through the night. Eventually, in his absolute exhaustion, he could move forward just one slow step at a time toward what he thought was his uncle . . . and

. . . hairy brown ducks with runny noses? Or was it big, screeching yellow eyes on muscular legs? Delusional, Rol plodded on as dark night gave way to even darker night, and then to a day-greeting sunrise—which he did not see because he was facedown on a manicured path, his eyes and mind closed to the world.

CHAPTER 6

PEANUT SHELLS AND PUDDING

Three days later, Rol woke up in a strange bed, a strange room, and an even stranger house. It was the house of one of Master DaTerrin's neighbors, Old Mrs. Crumblepockets. *The* Old Mrs. Crumblepockets.

Although Rol had never been inside the elder neighbor's unusual not-mansion, he was quite definitely there now. He had seen various views of the house's exterior, and those views obviously related to the room in which he currently resided. *Obviously related* was a bit of an understatement, actually.

Two weeks ago, when Rol had passed by Old Mrs. Crumblepockets' house . . . er, shack . . . he had noticed—and *had noticed* is also a bit of an understatement in that he had been utterly and life-changingly shocked—that the outside was covered in peanut shells.

Peanut shells. And uncannily large ones at that. The largest peanut shells that Rol had ever had the great fortune to see, until just that moment, when it became obvious that Old Mrs. Crumblepockets saved the whoppers for the inside. And *covered in peanut shells* was also an understatement for the interior walls, which it turned out were made of the freakish peanut shells painstakingly sewn together, not just smothered with them. It was the kind of sight that makes you want to say "!" ("!" being a placeholder for any word or phrase that might come out of your mouth with the intensity and velocity of "Run!" or "Help!" or "For the love of Smitty Gasserhansen!").

As Rol lay on his back facing the ceiling, which, interestingly, was *not* made of peanut shells from some dark nightmare, he squinted and then rubbed his eyes at the sight of the sight before and above him. A ceiling made entirely of dried and salted eel innards. Icky, squishy parts that had once most likely been squirming along with the rest of the mush but now were not. Dried because, well, how else could you expect to keep the afternoon rain out? And salted just because they looked salted, although Rol did not actually taste one to find out for sure, even though he was strangely tempted to partake in an activity that would likely be too unpleasant to ever forget. As his mind was reeling and his eyeballs were facing up, Rol heard a sound on the floorboard behind him. (*Floorboard* in this case meaning floor-boar, and there was possibly a good, although genuinely puzzling, story behind that.)

It was Old Mrs. Crumblepockets. And she held a plate of treats in her venerable and yet surprisingly nimble and bear-like hands.

"Did not think you would be wakin' up. No, did not at all, after all dem days," slurred the generally female-looking neighbor. "No movin' in your hands, your eyes a-closed for such a long time. And the pokin' didn't help none."

Rol suddenly noticed that his left side hurt a bit more than he remembered having left it a few days ago.

"Did not think you would be wakin' up, young one . . . but you did. And here you are. Jes' look at you. Eyes movin' all open, prob'ly ready for eatin', eh?" She violently, and at the same time tenderly, shoved a large plate of homemade bite-size hairy creations into his still mostly asleep hands.

He looked at the plate in wonder, and his insides protested their empty state loud enough to shake peanut shells from the walls. Rol wanted to close his eyes and start over again. But his growling stomach forced him to attempt to taste one of the horrors d' oeuvres before him.

They actually weren't terrible tasting, once you got past

the fur. With his stomach wavering between thanking and cursing him for the meal, Rol was able to think more clearly. He couldn't remember much of what he thought was yesternight, although it was actually three days earlier, other than realizing that DaTerrin was gone. *Gone.* It sounded awful and felt even worse. He lowered his head to the pillow, if you could call it that, and fell into a teary-eyed restless sleep.

Waking later in the day, still emotionally and physically drained from the recent experience, he was able to sit up on the side of the bed. Old Mrs. Crumblepockets was nowhere to be seen or heard, and that suited Rol for the moment, although he was grateful for her hospitality. His head was spinning and the images in his mind were blurry, but he felt that at least someone cared enough to take care of him, and that was comforting.

Old Mrs. Crumblepockets continued to be gracious in her outpouring of care, and was as close or distant as Rol needed her to be. She realized the tremendous loss he had experienced, tuning in as he unconsciously relived the awful night in muttered words and indecipherable phrases. He burned with a high fever the first day, and sitting by his side holding a cool cloth to his head was more or less the best she could do for him. Her worm pudding helped some, too, although she just called it pudding, keeping the real name of the delicacy to herself so as not to bother the boy with unnecessary details.

Over the next couple of days Rol, didn't talk much to his hostess, and his thoughts didn't stray much from trying to determine what to do next. He clung to the hope he had inside, fighting the urge to feel sorry for himself. Without knowing it, Rol was growing emotionally and gaining coping skills he would use his entire life. He also made the decision to drop the *Old* from Mrs. Crumblepockets' name.

When he had gathered enough strength to leave the house—even though he was still not eating much, other than a few swallows of the tasty yet unnamed pudding—Rol thanked Mrs. Crumblepockets with bright flowers he had picked from outside his window as well as a hug that meant everything to her. It also meant that most likely she would never see him again, which brought tears of sorrow as well as joy. She would again be alone in the house, but her memories of the past few days and the knowledge that she had helped pull the younger through the difficult time would sustain her the rest of her life.

Rol headed out the door holding a wooden bowl of a week's worth of pudding—what was that wonderful taste?—in one hand and warmly waving good-bye with the other. It was time to move on, and for starters that meant going back to the place he called home for the past few years.

Rol hesitantly walked through the door to the House of the Master, as he had decided it should be named, placed the pudding on the kitchen table, went to his familiar room and bed, and slept a full day and night. It was the least he could do for himself after all he had been through.

While asleep he dreamt of grieving the loss of DaTerrin, which was basically what he was doing when awake. In his dreams it was at first a sad experience, but there was a definite turning point when Rol realized that he must forge on—and he did. There was a joy of sorts when he thought about the time he had spent with his uncle. And although he was sad at the loss, he was happy for having had the experience. He also somehow knew that DaTerrin was in a good place.

Rol awoke suddenly and sat up. The long rest had cleared his mind completely. He pulled himself from the comfort of his bed and knelt down beside it, with prayers that offered thanks and asked for guidance. Then he ate a big meal for the first time in what seemed like an eternity, bathed, and decided to have a look around the house. He entered DaTerrin's bedroom—*previous* bedroom—for a clue on how to "Be."

Digging through DaTerrin's bedroom was something of an ordeal. The best way to appreciate the experience would be to run, screaming, into a large stone wall. Or you might try to use words such as *painanoia* or *tornadoquake*—or simply call out "Grash!" Or you might just decide not to describe it at all and save everyone, including yourself, the headache. Rol had known, almost since the beginning, that his master was a wise and intelligent, if somewhat eccentric, man. A man who collected things, especially shoes. Basic footwear, nothing too fancy. He apparently just felt the need to have a seemingly endless supply of new shoes—or old, as long as they were new to him. Rol never questioned that trait, probably because he never really noticed the extent of the collection.

Rol had a difficult time emotionally when seeing many of the objects that were associated with his master, even though it had been days now since DaTerrin had been taken away. Rol had been waiting and hoping that his uncle would come back but had come to realize that the chances of that were very slim. Impossible, actually.

Sorting through the many items scattered around the bedroom, Rol was confused. Should he stay? Should he go? And if so, where? There was food in the house, but that would not last forever. Rol found a few coins while digging through the top drawer of DaTerrin's dresser, but those, too, would not last forever. He could sell items from the house, but how much could he make from a few robes and trinkets that probably had sentimental value but no real worth?

What was he supposed to do?

Rol could try to find his parents, but that seemed unthinkable—although deep down it felt that was what he should do. But he could only remember glimpses of where he had lived previously, and the terrain was confined to a relatively small area, as his family was not known to wander far from home. His parents and sisters never considered going to other lands, because everything they needed appeared to be within reach.

The only long trip Rol remembered was when his parents had brought him to DaTerrin's house. Unfortunately, Rol was very ill and suffering a high fever almost from the beginning of that journey. His parents almost turned around at one point because they were concerned that Rol might not survive. They were welcomed by his uncle, DaTerrin, but his parents stayed only a few days, just long enough to ensure that their son was healing. At the time of their leaving, Rol was still clouded by the illness. Although he was healthy enough to say good-bye to his parents, Rol was not able to ask the many questions he had for them. He wished now that he had been able to inquire about his eventual journey home, but he never had the chance.

Considering his options, Rol was sure that he was meant to go back to the village and his family, but it was almost too much to believe that would ever happen.

DaTerrin had mentioned that the trip home would be difficult but little else. The only other real clue that Rol had about his previous home was that it was in or near Mapina-something. He didn't remember whether that was the name of the land or . . .

A smile formed as Rol looked at his uncle's shoe collection, and it all came together. Mapinashu. *Map in a shoe.* It was too easy and somewhat ridiculous. Actually, quite ridiculous. Silly, almost. Silly, definitely. If there actually was a map in a shoe, it was one of the most . . . Rol caught himself making a big deal about this. It wasn't as though this was a turning point in his story, was it? He made his way to the shoes to find out.

CHAPTER 7

A COLLECTION OF FOOTWEAR

Rol stood looking down at a lineup of shoes and boots on the bedroom floor. They were different shapes and sizes, but almost every pair was plain, other than miscellaneous and sometimes mysterious scuff marks. To Rol's untrained eyes, one pair seemed to be similar to the pair next to it. He reached into the first shoe on the left, probing all the way to the toe area, but found nothing but dust and small clumps of dirt.

Disappointment.

The second shoe of the pair also produced the same nothing. More disappointment.

Again and again, Rol reached into the shoes in the long line. Each time, nothing. He glanced toward the end of the line and thought that there would of course be a map in the very last shoe. Wasn't that how things worked? Excited, he moved to the last shoe, closed his eyes, and reached in. Nothing again. Rol moved to the next shoe in line. Again, no map.

Rol sat down on the edge of his uncle's bed and scratched his head, even though he knew the gesture was a cliché activity to do when thinking. He stood up, looking back at the line of fourteen pairs of shoes and boots, but had forgotten where he left off. Rol decided to move backward from the right end, and having already tried the first and second shoes, he proceeded to reach into the third one.

Immediately, his hand touched something inside the shoe, which happened to be for the left foot. He pulled out a brown animal-hide pouch with something inside that clinked when the pouch was jostled. With trembling hands, Rol opened the pouch.

Inside was a handful of gold coins, treasure to his younger eyes. It must have been DaTerrin's stash of saving-for-a-rainy-day-or-a-long-arduous-trip money. Rol thought a few moments about his uncle and the times he sold his valuable rainfruit in the market. The money was probably from those sales. The coins would pay for journeying items that Rol had been thinking about for the past day or so, and he felt that somehow the coins were meant for him.

Rol reached down and picked up the right shoe of the pair. Without even putting his hand inside, he knew that something was tucked in the back. Rol proceeded to pull out a long tube of flat and hairless hide. His hands no longer trembling—been there, done that—he untied the leather strap wrapped around the rolled-up hide. Once unrolled, the hide revealed a crudely drawn map. Apparently, the "map in a shoe" he was looking for.

Restraining himself from focusing only on the map, Rol looked into the remaining shoes to make sure he wasn't missing anything. Finding nothing, other than more dirt and a wayward sock, he carried the coins and map to the eating table for a better look.

The unrolled map was about as tall as one of Rol's hands, with fingers spread and measuring from thumb tip to pinky tip. It was twice as wide. The scrawlings on the map appeared to have been created by the burnt end of a thin stick. On the left end was something that almost resembled a house. Next to it was a single word—*Home*. Next to other basic drawings on the map, scattered along a winding path, were other words, apparently describing what was to be found there: *Horribly Disturbing Mountains, Forest of Painful Pricklyfeelythings, River of Don't,* among others. Most of those places were on the left side of the map. Toward the top middle and right side of the map, the words and symbols became scarcer except for a drawing on the right side. It, too, was a shape that appeared to be a house though without any label beside it.

Rol found it interesting that the map featured another route along the bottom that seemed much more direct. The path led through small towns and a few natural obstacles, but it generally appeared to be the shortest and best way from one house to the other.

Rol left the map on the table and returned to it often over the next few days while he was organizing and preparing. He understood that the map represented the plan for his future—at least for the time being. One area labeled as *Breathtaking Mountains* sounded promising, and Rol held on to that thought.

One night, soon after he discovered the map, Rol woke up in a panic.

"Be?" he thought. That was what he was supposed to do for the rest of his life? What exactly did "Be" mean? What did one do while "Be"ing? Why should he be the one to "Be"? He couldn't get the "Be" questions out of his head, which was clouded and on the verge of, well, *being* terribly fuzzy. DaTerrin said "Be" as if it was a perfectly normal thing to say to your only friend as your last word.

"Be" he said, and what he said was "Be." It was exactly

"Be," and not even a little more . . . of anything else. Or less, although one couldn't have said much less. Not ". . . yourself" or ". . . true to yourself" or even ". . . a man." What was it with "Be"? It made absolutely no sense. And yet it made nothing but sense. DaTerrin, his beloved friend and master, his adviser for all things, the wisely one, the old hoot owl, the usually-distracted-and-most-often-confusing-and-yet-once-in-a-while-perfectly-sensible-and-mentally-aware sage had said . . . "Be."

In the end, Rol had no choice. He could do something and "Be," or do nothing and not do anything. Which is to say, Rol actually *did* have a choice, although the one that involved doing "nothing" didn't sound fulfilling as a life. Rol decided then and there that he would "Be." Whatever that meant.

It seemed a perfectly good occasion for the triumphant blare of magnificently glorious trumpets resounding in unison to mark the life-changing moment.

Yet there was nothing. Such the luck.

CHAPTER 8

FIFTY FEET (NO MORE, NO LESS)

Days later, Rol decided it was time to get on with his great adventure, to reunite with his family. His semi-hasty, but also well-thought-out plan was to go soon, before the weather turned for the worse in the seasons ahead. Rol had a general sense of a few important items to pack, but he wasn't experienced in terms of taking long journeys—and so he was somewhat at a loss as to how to proceed.

After looking around Master DaTerrin's cottage for items he thought might be appropriate to take, Rol piled some on the floor in the main living area and leaned others against one of the bare walls. That way, everything was laid out and he could get an idea of what he had and what he needed. He would then figure out how to make it all work on his long trek.

Rol made a quick checklist of things that seemed to be missing. He needed to be careful not to overload himself. He also didn't want to *under*load himself, only to later regret he had failed to bring along something important, such as an extra pair of comfy socks or a fashionable yet functional traveling hat. Rol wouldn't be traveling by horseback. And because taking a mule along was not part of the plan, he would be carrying his pack and any other items he might need. Rol was fairly strong and agile for his age, but the journey would be long, which meant he could take only items that were truly necessary. Otherwise he wouldn't get far. Or far enough.

With a scrawled list of various items he still needed in hand, Rol headed to the market in town. He was intent on finding a small shop that he had passed recently when gathering food items. He paused for a moment, reflecting. *That was the day I tried to pull the magic duck egg prank on Uncle.*

The small shop looked like a tiny trading post from the outside, but once Rol walked through the wide and disconcertingly crumbling doorway, he found himself in a large and well-stocked room. Rol strode in purposefully and, nodding customer-like to the shop owner, began looking around. Glancing over wooden boxes and around precariously perched piles of things and through stacks of unrecognizable clothing items and under hanging whatsits, he noticed equipment that seemed to be exactly what he was looking for. In a corner, he spotted coiled and uncoiled lengths of rope, comfortable-looking and yet probably inordinately expensive traveling clothes, blankets, cloaks, hats, walking sticks, and even a few weapons. All seemingly waiting just for him.

Standing in the corner area dumbfounded, Rol started by sorting through the ropes to determine which one to purchase. While wondering what he would actually do as the proud new owner of a rope, he felt a hand tapping his right shoulder. Turning his which-rope-do-I-really-need glance to his right, he did not see anyone. Rol quickly realized that the tapping person was on his left and had reached over to tap his right shoulder—an old but still funny joke. It was the shop owner he had nodded to a few moments before.

Surprised at someone standing so close to him—having possibly snuck up on him, Rol turned toward the shop owner while also backing away from him a couple of steps. He hoped that having a little space between them would make their conversation more comfortable. The shop owner, though, had other ideas. He took two steps forward, closing the space, and talked to Rol in a rush, filling his ears and mind with information that couldn't possibly be absorbed so quickly.

As the shop owner bombarded Rol with information about "must have for the well-equipped traveler" products and "I bet you didn't realize" descriptions and "lower than low" low prices, Rol took in the overall appearance of the man. He looked well traveled and slightly haggard, though he seemed friendly and well meaning. Although not quite as tall as Rol, he was much heavier and broader. His choice of clothes somehow signaled "former adventurer." They appeared to be well fitting and suited for action, even though they were wearing thin and had been hastily repaired in places. The man's face was etched by many years of journeying from here to there and back again, with warm smiles for newly found friends and scowls for unwelcoming locals along the way. Dark hair, sun-darkened skin, interesting scars on face and hands, uneven yellow-tinged teeth, and an interesting accent rounded out the physical traits of the man who owned the local adventure-seeking shop. And apparently the shop was exactly that, as Rol had just noticed the sign on a wall announcing "Local Adventure-Seeking Shop" in large, handwritten letters, with the *S* facing backward on the word *Shop*.

While talking, the shop owner attempted to gauge Rol's interest in particular products and sell him what he deemed appropriate for his journey, but also, in a bit of self-interest, old items that the shop owner was anxious to sell before they gathered any more dust.

"Where you going, son? You going on a long trip? Going alone? What will you be doing on this trip? In which direction are you going? Do you have somebody or something to help you carry all the things you wish to take? Do you have the correct type of pack? Do you have the proper boots? Have you considered a fashionable yet functional traveling hat? How long will you be gone, and what weather do you expect to encounter?" There were questions upon questions upon questions that made Rol dizzy, his head spinning with all the possibilities ahead and all the inquiries that he could not possibly answer completely or correctly.

The shop owner quickly gathered that Rol was not an experienced traveler, and was really counting on his help. A little smile spread across his face—one that Rol was not sure how to take. However it appeared, it was actually a change-of-heart smile, which can be difficult to recognize, even by the supposed experts.

The rough, worn, once-full-of-great-adventure-and-bravery shop owner felt compassion for Rol because he looked lost and obviously did not have the answers to the questions that had been posed. This shop owner, who had experienced many things in his life, now had a choice: He could take advantage of the situation and try to sell Rol items that he didn't need, or he could truly help him.

Very quickly the choice was made to help equip Rol with what he needed, instead of selling him outdated things that would essentially be useless to him a day or two after he left the shop. It was a lucky break for Rol, who felt that the man was on his side. Instinctively, he truly trusted the shop owner, believing he had found someone who would prove to be extremely valuable in helping him kick off his long journey—which is exactly what he needed at a time when he had so many questions himself.

Recalling the intimidating-looking mountains on the map, Rol decided the climbing supplies section would be a good place to start, and that is when Mr. Shop Owner began to provide genuine assistance.

"Rope? Looking for rope?" he asked. "Well, I have a great selection here. Really, an unmatched selection anywhere in these parts. Actually, I believe I'm known for my rope selection in all the surrounding towns. No joke. I know my stuff when it comes to ropes. And you need fifty feet of that, my young traveler."

"Why fifty feet, older shop owner?" asked Rol.

"Because anyone who's going on any journey of any significance needs fifty feet of rope—everyone knows that."

"I didn't know that," retorted Rol.

"Well, let me rephrase that," continued the owner of the shop. "Everyone who is serious about traveling and knows anything about it knows that. By the way, I think we've known each other long enough now that you should call me something other than shop owner. My name is Anthonononsense the Adventure-Seeker, but you can call me Adventure-Seeker, or Anthon the shop owner, or just Anthon."

"Pleased to meet you, Anthon," said Rol, "and my name is Rol, the Just-Now-Adventure-Seeker, or just Rol. Now, about this fifty feet of rope business. Why fifty feet? Why not twenty-five feet?"

"I could spend days educating you about the storied history of rope carrying, but let me just simplify it down to: Because fifty feet is what you need. We'll leave it at that."

"I appreciate your wisdom, Anthon, but why not one hundred feet?"

"Because I'm telling you, you need *fifty* feet."

"I'm not a rope expert—that we've made clear. But it appears that you sell varying lengths of rope, as noted earlier in this scene. Is that true?"

"I do have varying lengths of rope, apparently as noted earlier by someone when you walked in, although I wasn't paying much attention at that point, but fifty feet of rope is what I'm telling you that you need."

"Even though I haven't told you anything about where I'm going or for how long?"

"I don't need to know any more details for the rope recommendation. I knew immediately when you walked in through my disconcertingly crumbling doorway. 'Fifty feet of rope is what that one needs,' I said to myself."

"So I really don't have a choice in this?" questioned Rol.

"You do have a choice, but I'm afraid that anything other than what I recommend in rope would be, quite frankly, a terrible and possibly life-threatening mistake," answered Anthon confidently. "Although I have a large selection of choices, each item is not for every occasion. You tell me what type of journeying you are planning, I tell you what you should take. Except the rope. I know that early on, before any speaking even takes place. I find this all works the best for the customer, so that's how I operate. Deal? And when you have finalized your purchase—since you have bought rope and all—I will show you some knots I have found to be most useful out in the wilderness."

The next several moments consisted of Rol describing his situation, Anthon asking more questions—slowly and one at a time now—and then waiting for the answers, also one at a time. Two potential customers entered the shop at some point, seeking Anthon's recommendation on rope, but he dismissed them with an "I'm busy" look as he focused on Rol. There were more questions still, followed by a rustling and efficient assembling of traveling items specifically chosen for Rol. Done.

"How would you like to pay for these, fellow adventure-seeker?" asked Anthon.

A short time later, Rol exited the shop and gazed around the market for other necessary traveling items. He ran into a younger who was slightly older than Rol, technically making him an older younger, which is ridiculous enough that it will not be mentioned again—probably. The two had met in town a few months prior and had talked briefly about going fishing or rock skimming by the village pond, but for some reason it never happened.

"Are you going down to The Mace tonight?" asked the boy. "They will have live music."

Rol wondered what other kind of music there was. He shrugged and said, "I don't know." For the record, it actually sounded more like "I ohhnoh," but that doesn't come across as well unless you are actually talking to another boy your age.

Having nothing else to say, they parted ways.

While still considering the question about The Mace, Rol walked around the village center in search of anything else he might need for his journey. It was best for him to assume he could rely solely on what he would be carrying. He didn't know whether he would happen upon other towns, and even if there were some, there was no way to know what if any supplies would be available. Rol hoped that he would meet people along the way, and that they would be friendly and welcoming—but he could not count on either. It was reasonable to think that there might be fruit trees along the way, which would be handy in an emergency. Still, it would be wiser for him to get used to eating light and stocking up when he could.

After picking up food for the trip that would keep well and remain semi-tasty for a few days, Rol wandered past The Mace. The drinking and eating establishment was technically for all ages, although the very young were discouraged from entering after dark because that would likely put them in danger of someone falling on them at some point during the night. Rol had never been inside The Mace. When he and DaTerrin had passed by it on occasion, the master consistently tried to distract Rol from seeing the unsavory townsfolk who busily entered and exited the building. Rol liked the wooden sign over the door that had a crude but bold painting of a metal mace, spikes and all, as well as a warning about being fallen upon, or words to that effect but less grammatically correct. It was not a busy time of day, and Rol heard only a light bustle coming from inside. It was enough to pique his interest now that he was alone, and he crossed the threshold into the dark and misty pub, his pack of supplies on his back.

Lit torches lined the walls. Tables and chairs were scattered throughout the place. A large area in one corner was elevated slightly, and unlit torches surrounded what Rol recognized as a stage. Steps led up to it, and for the time being it was empty of performers or stagehands.

Some people, who might have been workers, moved around the place carrying trays back and forth and moving chairs from one end of a table to another. To Rol it appeared they were attempting to look busy. He was regarded with a nod or a smile, but nobody stopped to inquire about his needs or intent.

Suddenly, from out of the shadows to Rol's right, a tall man approached him. The man rested one hand on Rol's shoulder while reaching out with the other to shake the younger's hand in the proper greeting manner.

"Glad to see you, my boy. Glad to see you," said the fast-talking elder, slapping at Rol's new pack and smiling broadly with every word uttered. "I see you brought the mystery instrument. Can't wait to hear it. But first, can I get you anything?"

"No. No, thank you," said Rol slowly, unsure what the exchange was about. "But I think you . . ."

"Can't wait to hear it," said the man again, "and by the way, I'm the pub's promoter, Fhil, but you can call me Fh. That's where you'll be." He motioned toward the stage. "When is everyone else arriving? I didn't catch your name, Mr. . . ."

"My name is Rol, not Mr. *Anything*. I don't know who everyone else is, or what a promoter is. I'm sorry, but . . ."

"And that's it? Rol? That's your name, then?" questioned the new acquaintance, Fh, placing his right finger on his chin in a thoughtful manner as he thought, without looking up to see Rol nodding.

"Rol, Rol . . . Rol," Fh said to himself while ignoring Rol, who was standing in front of him—and who was bewildered by the goings-on around him. The previously busy-looking chair shufflers were now busy looking at Rol.

"If you don't mind, *Rol*, why don't we go with *Ro* for you from now on. You know, as your stage name."

"Why not *Rol*? That's my name."

"Yes, but, you have to have a stage name. So people can identify with you."

"But my name is Rol. People can identify with that."

"Yes, but, you see, Ro is very, you know, *now*. Rol is, you know, not."

"Rol is a great name. It's my name. Anyway, I don't want to have a stage name."

"But if you don't have a stage name, it's practically purposeless to be onstage, really."

"That's the point."

"Yes, but . . . Anyway, we'll talk about that later," said Fh, ending the conversation for the moment by walking toward one of the workers who was shuffling tables and chairs around, this time for an even less apparent reason, and complaining loudly about those in the crowd who would make his life difficult that night by moving the furniture wherever they wanted anyway. Rol heard a few words he did not want to hear and saw a few hand gestures he did not want to see.

He took advantage of the moment and slinkily backed out of The Mace, never to return.

CHAPTER 9

ON THE RIGHT PATH?

Rol made his way back to his uncle's cottage without further distractions. Alone now, he was looking for his place in the world. A place where he belonged. At least a place where he *felt* he belonged. Interestingly, he didn't actually feel uncomfortable anywhere, so it was almost as though he belonged anywhere—or even everywhere. But he knew he didn't belong where he was just then, because he felt a distinct longing for somewhere else that was yet to be determined.

The map he had left on the table would guide him. That he knew, and that would cure the ever-longing, somehow. The destination of his journey was not exactly known, but it was a safe bet to assume it would be . . . somewhere. And a fairly-to-somewhat-safe bet to assume it was where he belonged, or at least would belong. DaTerrin had the map for a reason—that was certain, and Rol was sure that reason involved him.

Struggling to get the thoughts of truly belonging somewhere, anywhere, out of his mind, Rol reviewed the map closely once again. With a finger, he traced one of the distinct paths on the map. The trail started on the left at the crude drawing labeled *Home* that could have been a house, if one were to squint and reach into the depths of his or her imagination while considering it. There were words and symbols leading from that *Home* drawing to another but unlabeled drawing that was possibly a house on the right side, the east, almost at the edge of the map. That path led in an almost direct line across the map, and appeared to be the most direct route. Simple enough.

The other path meandered in an arc toward the top of the map—north—and then back down to the same destination as the other route. The longer path had more colorful names as landmark descriptions along the way and certainly appeared to be a much more difficult journey. Each time he viewed the map and contemplated following the indirect route, his impression was always the same. And why would he have thought otherwise? From approximately halfway along that route to the end, there were no more symbols, no more words, no more clues. There were words and symbols leading to major landmarks along the way, but the trail itself led into areas marked only by strange symbols. After that there were empty areas that would most likely be recognizable only by the curves of the dashed line on the map, indicating hills or mountains or waterways. It was as if the mapmaker did not finish his work because he did not know what was there. The terrain would likely become more difficult there, and Rol would be facing it alone.

Rol had a choice to make.

Which way to go—the easier way, so clearly marked on the map for him, or the difficult route that included so many unknowns and would take much longer? Rol was not an experienced traveler, so the straight path was the logical choice. Anyway, why would he delay getting to his home, which he believed was indicated by the drawing to the east?

His uncle said the journey would be arduous. The straight path didn't look arduous, but Rol would be alone, and that could make any traveling more difficult, right? The discussion in Rol's mind went back and forth. The easy way? Or the difficult way? What if the so-called easy way was not so easy but actually much more difficult? What if Rol was hurt along the way and needed help? Help wouldn't come on a route that was not traveled, and Rol could end up stuck in a dire situation. What about food, since he could only carry so much? What about his parents and sisters, who were maybe waiting for him?

Interestingly enough, if Rol had let his imagination wander a little more, he might have thought about the possibility of invisible runes marked on the map that would help guide him. Invisible runes that would become visible only by holding the map up to a full moon on certain nights of the year—and only if the map holder was standing in a certain position, in a specific location, allowing the light of the moon to reveal symbols and helpful words from the celestial illumination on the back of the tattered yet fully functional map. Runes that were put there by an elder of an ancient and long-forgotten race, an elder who happened to be extremely gifted at that sort of thing. Runes that would change Rol's life forever, as they would reveal the secrets of his destiny.

Fortunately, Rol didn't consider that sort of nonsense, which spared him from wasting time and mental energy on fretting over something that wasn't actually real. It turned out to be fortunate for him, because at that potentially imagination-wasting moment . . .

Someone knocked on the door.

It was Anthon, a pleasant interruption for Rol. The shop owner presented Rol with a traveling hat, saying that he wanted the soon-to-be-journeyer to travel in style and comfort, and the newly made hat offered both. Since Rol had made a large purchase in the adventure store, Anthon thought it only right that Rol should have the hat free of charge. He apologized for not thinking of the gift sooner, as well as for his delay in finding out where Rol lived.

Rol was still caught up in the middle of choosing a path decision. Seizing the opportunity to solicit an informed opinion, he asked Anthon a question about his life.

"You've obviously been on many journeys, and I'm sure that some were easier than others," said Rol. "But in the end . . . well, you're here. You made it. How did you make it through the travels that were not so easy?"

Anthon took a moment to reflect. He scratched his scruffy chin. He smiled. He scratched again.

"Sometimes you don't know what you're made of," Anthon said. "A situation may present itself and then you have a choice: move forward or stop, maybe retreat. You must consider your options carefully, but don't wait too long. And don't talk yourself out of something even though it may be a challenge. And, as a side note, don't talk to yourself too much, unless you're sure you're alone. It all probably sounds like a schooling lesson, but sometimes you have to take a risk to get the most reward. I don't know if that answers your question or helps any, but that's the way I see it. That's what gets me through."

"It helps," replied Rol. "Thank you, and thank you for the hat. I'm sure it will come in handy."

Anthon left, wishing him Godspeed.

The next day, Rol left his uncle's house. He locked up everything as best he could, gazed one final time at the house and surrounding land, and started walking. He passed by Mrs. Crumblepockets, who was on her doorstep, shaking out a rug made of . . . fish scales? Rol waved heartily, and she waved back warmly. As he moved along the path and beyond the village limits, he said to himself, "What a grand adventure this is! Wonderful weather. I love being outdoors."

After three days, with too-frequent resting periods becoming a habit, he was still walking. Rol said loudly, "A terrible misadventure this is. Entirely. I don't like being outdoors any longer. I want to be somewhere else. This is quite possibly the biggest mistake I have ever made. May I go back now?"

After another day of walking, Rol reached the point on the map where the path split, affording two choices: easy and difficult. Those specific options weren't noted on the map, of course, or on the actual pathway. However, there was a wooden sign on the side of the road that indicated: *This way is best.* And as he expected, it pointed in the direction of the route that looked easier on the map.

Rol could continue in only one direction. The easy path looked well traveled. The difficult path did not. Pausing for just a few rapid heartbeats, he semi-confidently headed toward the north. It was precisely what he had planned to do after thinking the past few days about what Anthon had said and then sleeping on the decision—quite literally using the rolled-up map as a pillow. He hoped the risk would pay off, and he felt that DaTerrin might have somehow challenged him to take that path over the other, although it appeared his master was giving him the freedom to choose. It would be difficult for Rol to get back on the easy path once he had committed to the other. He could always turn around, retrace his steps, and resume on the easy path at a later date, although he didn't believe that was in his life plan. With towns and villages along the way, there was also a chance that he would come across other routes that could lead him back to the easy path. But Rol considered that only a fall-back position should his travels turn dire at some point.

As he headed north, Rol at first thought that the route didn't seem particularly difficult. There were no ominous clouds in the distance, with lightning and darkness signaling hard times ahead. In fact, stopping to consider the two routes some more provided some relief. The path was of the same flatness, with a hint of the distant mountains ahead. The scattered trees looked to be basically the same types. The sky overhead was a nice shade of blue.

While walking and reading the map, Rol realized that

following a wayfinder was not a simple matter. He had no way of knowing exactly where the landmarks would be, other than moving in what he believed to be the general direction and then happening upon them, recognizing an area by the way it was detailed on the map, or asking someone. Since leaving his uncle's cottage a few days before, he had come across only a handful of travelers, and those encounters had been on a main route, so he did not expect much company along the way of his own journey. Rol also realized that his would be a journey of many months. His insides felt funny. Excited and anxious, terrified and worried. Rol tucked the map inside his backpack for easy retrieval, knowing that he would rely on it frequently.

More walking, and he was still at it two days later. And two days after that. And four days after that. His pace was steady. That said, Rol stopped multiple times to rest or camp for the night, taking advantage in the first few days of just about every item he had bought from Anthon—even the hat a couple of times when it rained. He also stopped occasionally when he came across a wondrous sight that invited him to remain for a few moments. Mountains, hills, valleys, streams, tame and wild animals, clouds, and sunsets were all glorious reminders of a blessed life. He had not yet reached any of the landmarks shown on the map, but he still believed that he was going in the right direction—and that he would encounter something noted soon. Doing so would be a relief, as it would confirm his innate sense of direction, which he questioned at times. Rol walked another day in the amazing outdoors.

And then, nothing happened . . . again.

Since nothing of major interest was happening to Rol as he traveled from where he was to where he was going, he decided that he should stir up something exciting. Hopefully, that something would build into an avalanche of excitement, which at its peak could not be reduced, much less stopped. Getting in the way of the excitement avalanche would be to no avail, and that was fine with Rol, who just wanted something, *anything*, to happen instead of having to endure more of the monotony of his legs moving forward. Oh, and sometimes moving backward and sideways, too. Can't forget those. That would be like forgetting something that was incredibly exciting, and there was nothing that was as exciting as thinking about exciting things that could possibly happen, some way, somehow, sometime. It was *exciting* just to think about being excited! Excited. Excited, excited, excited. After the word was said or even thought a few times, it lost its meaning. *Excited.* To Rol it didn't even sound like a real word any longer. Excited? No, not real. Gibberish. Like the word *gibberish*, which sounded full of gibberishness. Or is it gibberishocity? *Excited.* Eggsited, ecksited, "Echh sighted!" No, still not real.

Rol paused for a moment when he realized he was in a swamp. "How did I get here?" he puzzled, as he stood there. In the swamp.

CHAPTER 10

UNIQUELY SPECIAL

It probably wasn't the smartest place to be. Rol was by himself, and he was not good at finding his way out of swamps. He made it a point to stay away from the smelly, nasty places when at all possible, which was always. In fact, he had never been in a real swamp before. Since this was his first time, and because he was swamp challenged, or at least less experienced swamp-wise than most everyone else, he should not have done the one thing that someone with swamp experience would know not to do, which was to walk straight in, unaccompanied. Alone. In the soon-to-be dark.

But he did do just that, and eventually made it through the experience unscathed and basically having not learned anything more about swamps than he knew when he first walked in.

"So much for that!" he exclaimed to absolutely no one in the general vicinity. "That was rather uneventfully less nasty than I expected." And he went about his travels unconfounded.

When you are traveling alone on the path of life, as Rol was, it doesn't take long to realize how alone you are on said path of life. Even if being alone is for only a few days, as it was in Rol's case so far, it can still feel like a long time. It was a definite journey down the path of life for Rol, and so it was important for him to ponder it appropriately.

Rol sat down on the next comfortable-looking log to think about time passing and to take a break. And to eat some crackly spindle-crackers, his favorite sit-down-and-rest snack. And drink warm water, which was all he had, though at that point he was grateful for anything to wash down the flavorful crackers he loved, but had forgotten just how oh-so-dry they were.

Refreshed, Rol continued down the path of life, which he at that moment decided to officially call Pancreas for no good reason other than it made him giggle when he said it. And the other possible reason, which was that he thought he remembered having an Aunt Pancreas at one time. She might have been the one who introduced him to crackly spindle-crackers.

Nine days later, Rol clearly remembered that his aunt was, in fact, not Aunt Pancreas but Aunt Lungpickle. He decided to continue to call his traveling down the path of life Pancreas anyway, which made him giggle still, although nobody else understood why.

Walking, walking, walking. Pick up one foot, put it down. Pick up the other, put it down. It was mindless work, and Rol's mind wandered. Of course, back to the time with his uncle but also to earlier times.

Rol had very good memories of his time with Master DaTerrin. Beyond being his uncle, DaTerrin was a good person and a friend, eventually, even though at the beginning of that new life, Rol wanted no part of him or the life that was suddenly his to live.

Rol had been taken to DaTerrin at a young age with the explanation that DaTerrin, a wise and respected man, would take care of him until Rol became wiser himself. The assumption for the arrangement did not hold much promise from Rol's perspective, as he did not believe that he was considered wiser-possible by those around him. That disbelief was in part because of his age, as it was rare for any younger to be considered wise, but also due to the fact that Rol was, and always had been, a free spirit. He was about as serious as a playful otterling and could rarely sit still even long enough to eat an average meal, which was far too little time for him to concentrate and learn much about the ways of the world.

Still, people in Rol's village said that there was something special about him. They said it as a compliment without overdoing it, so as to keep Rol from becoming prideful or boastful. On the contrary, whenever Rol received that compliment—although it was vague and never followed up by much explanation, other than the person saying that Rol would do something important one day—his face would turn reddish, indicating that he felt he did not deserve the description and that he had no good response.

On one occasion, when an elder woman said the word "unique" when looking at him, Rol asked bluntly, "What is meant by that? What do you mean by saying that there is something unique about me?"

The woman who spoke the word looked at Rol in the oddest way and said thoughtfully, "I don't know exactly. It is something I can't put into words. I just feel it and I almost see it about you, as though there were a cloak of light of some sort wrapped around you and causing you to glow slightly."

And then, after a long pause from her as she reflected, came the word "special," followed by a slight shaking of her head and a squinting of her eyes. It was as if the elder woman was trying to form the words that would better describe the phrase but could only muster a mysterious feeling. This reaction occurred on several occasions. Rol was conflicted, what with being a younger who was mostly concerned about his own ways but also one who spent some time each day thinking about the rest of the world. What difference did it make what other people thought? They seemed unable to explain what they thought about him anyway. What did they know, and why would he care?

Rol realized, though, that he *did* care. He remembered asking another elder in the village about the words and what they could mean, and he was told that he would understand soon enough. Sent on his way with a trio of off-you-go pats on the head was not enlightening at all, and left Rol feeling good about himself but also in need of answers.

It was interesting to Rol that he did not remember DaTerrin ever mentioning the words "unique" or "special" about him at any time. The master used, and used often, references such as "Something else," "Something not of this world," and "Something that the skrat dragged in" to describe his feelings about Rol. Thinking them playful phrases, Rol did not take them as negative and, instead, thought they were probably meant to instill humility. He still wondered, though, and wondered often, where his life was leading.

Rol's mind was spinning with all the "unique" and "special" thinking he had been doing. And just when he began to think he was too weary to take even one more step, he walked out of a forest and into a clearing. He had not expected to encounter anything significant so soon. His heart started to beat faster with excitement.

Boredom, be gone! At least temporarily.

CHAPTER 11

CONFUSION, ENLIGHTENMENT— AND TASTY, TOO

Rol walked right up to a large tented area in the clearing. As expected, it was filled with large tents. Large grayish tents to be exact. Interestingly enough, thought Rol, the entire area appeared to be deserted, which was odd on a late sunny afternoon when the air was so pleasant.

Rol scanned the scene before him and noticed that the nearest tent had a flap, with two wooden signs craftily sewn onto it. One neatly read: "Guaranteed or Your Money Back." The other beside it just as neatly read: "Thank you for coming to the psychic fair. You had a great time. That will be three silver pieces. Pay as you leave, which is right here. No, over to the left. A little more. Right there. Thank you and good-bye."

Rol didn't know what to do, so he put three small silver pieces in a slot to the left of the sign and was about to walk away when he stopped suddenly . . . and thought. He thought a bit longer. Then he thought just one moment more to try to make sense of what had just happened. He had just paid what to him was two weeks' wages for having received . . . nothing. At least that's what he thought he thought. It was just that the sign was convincingly matter-of-fact and made it impossible not to pay, so he felt compelled to pay, even though, obviously, he had never been there prior to that exact moment. And hadn't even realized until the convincing sign informed him where he was that he was anywhere near a psychic fair, whatever that was.

Rol felt cheated and surprisingly disappointed in himself. Not having money to waste—and valuing those three coins, which were now apparently not his any longer because of the slot having been well-constructed so as to prevent an arm reaching through it to extract coins or any other objects—he decided to ask for his money back.

With the full pack on his back, sans the three silver pieces, and his handy Battlestick in his right hand but held as a walking stick so as not to intimidate unnecessarily, Rol strode into the vacant encampment.

He found it rather . . . empty. No movement. No sound.

No psychics, whatever they were. Rol walked the area for quite some time, looking in and around all the tents. Seeing that there was nothing to see, he headed back toward the faux welcome center in search of his silver. Just before reaching the backside of the tent that had started it all, he heard a light hum, as though someone was humming a light tune that had carried playfully on the wind.

Rol walked closer to the first tent he had approached earlier—the large gray one that held his coins. He saw a shadow moving on the side of the tent and called out loudly, "Is anyone here?"

The humming stopped. The answer was . . . silence.

Rol knew that he had heard and seen *something*, so he walked to the front of the tent and asked again. This time there was a shuffling noise inside but still no reply. Rol tried to find an opening by grabbing the tent and pulling the material in different places to reveal a way in. A small section opened up, and he could just barely poke his head inside for a peek. It was not the smartest thing to do, but he did it anyway.

Inside the large tent was a large amount of empty space. A small wooden table was at its center—with a very small pile of three coins next to a pouch on it—along with a crude wooden chair and a man in a brightly colored robe, who was seated in it with one side to Rol.

The man turned in his chair and saw Rol. He then turned away from him and started to nervously push the coins into the pouch. He pulled the hood of his robe up over his head. He sat very still, evidently trying not to move. Rol could still hear him breathe.

Rol said honestly, “I can still hear you breathe.”

The man took a deep breath and then held it. A few moments went by. A few more. The man let out the deep breath. He quickly breathed in deeply and held his breath again.

Rol said truthfully, “And I can still see you.”

The man let out his breath, then climbed down under the table. He pulled his hood up even further over his head and took in another deep breath.

Rol said, frustrated, “Look. I just want my coins back. I can see you and hear you. Why don’t you toss me my three coins, and you can go back to what you were doing.”

The man appeared to think about this. He crawled out from under the table, pulled his hood back, brushed himself off, and approached the area where Rol was peeking through the hole in the tent. The man walked right past Rol, and then out through a large opening on the tent’s side. Rol pulled his head back. The man walked up to him, held out the three coins, and dropped them into Rol’s now outstretched hand.

“We’re closed,” is all the man said. Taking down the

signs, he started shuffling away.

Rol said to the man's back, "By the way, your sign was wrong. I didn't have a great time. In fact, it was not even a good time. But I wish you well."

The man muttered something about it always ending up that way, which is why everyone left. He said he was always giving back money. Sullenly, the man walked away, leaving Rol more confused than when he arrived.

On his own and walking again.

After the "psychic fair" experience, Rol recalled times with his uncle. As he grew in years and in his ability to comprehend the lessons his uncle taught, the teachings had become more challenging. DaTerrin often questioned his nephew on topics they had previously discussed, to ensure that they were taken in properly: How does a tree produce fruit? What is the meaning of the word *ambition*? Describe three possible methods to handle a situation involving two townsfolk quarreling over a stream that runs through both of their properties. DaTerrin also introduced new concepts such as forgiveness, loyal opposition, and reverence.

The latter sparked further conversation.

"Uncle, I don't understand," said Rol one afternoon. "Some people believe in one God. I have heard that others believe in many gods. Is there really more than one?"

"More than one doesn't make sense to me at all," replied DaTerrin.

"But how do you know?"

"Try this. Close your eyes. Now when I say *gods*, what do you see in your mind?"

"OK. Hmmm . . . I see many faces. They are talking. Arguing, actually. They are trying to decide which of them is best. Arguing, and even fighting."

"Now open your eyes. Count to ten, then close them again. Good. What if I say *God*?"

"I don't see anything. Wait . . . I see a face. It is my father. No . . . my mother. No, it is you. It is all of you in one face, but also the face of someone I don't think I have seen before. Someone who is smiling."

"I can't see in your mind, just as I can't see through your eyes," said DaTerrin. "You must decide what you believe based on what you learn and experience. I think that smile is a good place to begin."

The reflection led Rol to consider his beliefs, and his actions according to those beliefs. He had a long time to reflect, and his thoughts kept him company through the days of his journey.

One afternoon, Rol hiked through an incredibly green and lush forest. There was no discernible path, but the walking was easy because the trees and bushes were spread apart enough to pass through them comfortably. At least in the beginning. Rol stopped for awhile to eat, resting on a downed tree that served as a nice bench.

It was cool in the forest, with a light breeze rustling the leaves high above Rol. He could have easily passed the day away in the place, without missing the walking in the slightest. But alas, the journey beckoned.

Standing up and pulling his pack on again, Rol leaned against an old tree, which also started to lean and then crashed to the ground. Not thinking much of it, Rol tightened his pack for the walk ahead and took three steps. Two and a half, actually.

From out of the bushes they came, like furious hornets from a disturbed nest. Hundreds of biting, clawing creatures with painfully pointed fangs and talons as long as their gnarled forearms. Before he took off, Rol had just one chance to get a good look at the horde and a few of the individual creatures. Then he ran faster than he had ever run before—straight ahead, his legs digging and pushing and aching. Over ancient tree stumps, under snatching branches, and barely around boiling mud pools that should have claimed him, just as they sucked in some of his pursuers. But no matter which way he turned or ducked or jumped, still they came.

They were the ferocious Torg—the race of tiny beings no taller than the height of one of Rol's ears, though the nasty creatures could of course be measured accurately only if one of them actually stood still, which according to legend they never did. Each was far more dangerous than any rodent four or five times its size, even bleederats. They traveled in packs numbering as many as a thousand, and Rol was fortunate that this group was maybe a third of that size.

I thought the Torg were just a legend, Rol pondered, and pondered quickly as they continued their continuous chase. And if razor-sharp fangs in their mouths and talons at the ends of their hairy bat-like arm-wings were not enough, each Torg carried a sharp object for slicing or piercing. Some weapons were shards of crystal; others, splintered mahogany or ebony. They snarled in unison as they half ran and half flew, gaining on Rol with every tiny but purposeful lurch forward.

Rol breathed in gulps of mist as he ran almost blindly through the muggy forest. The mist made his lungs burn even more, as the stuff was not the true air that he needed to fill his airways and help maintain his pace. He hoped that the damp air was having the same effect on the dreaded little Torg imps. Even so, he could not pause to worry in the slightest about them and continued to bob and weave his way through the even denser forest with its vines that whipped his skin raw as he ran.

Rol kept his eyes peeled for any sign of a cliff that he both hoped and feared would be in sight soon, according to the map and his decent but sometimes questionable sense of direction. He had heard stories that the Torg never pursue their prey over the side of a cliff because they're afraid of heights, so the so-called Cliffs of Largeish Heights would be welcomed right about then—as long as there was a safe way down them, as opposed to a free fall onto jagged rocks below as his only means of escape.

Rol heard the nightmarish snarling fade as though he was outdistancing them, but he did not want to get his hopes up. He knew they were bloodthirstily relentless and would not give up that easily. Though weary, Rol continued on another thirty bounds until he thought his lungs would burst. He realized that the cliffs he had counted on were not as close as he hoped. Then, with a painful though oddly welcome crash into a wet and uncomfortably sticky plant the size of DaTerrin's cottage, Rol's mad dash came to an end.

Trying desperately not to make a sound as he gasped and gulped, Rol listened intently for any sound, any trace of the Torg. But instead of the snarlings of hundreds of tiny, fiendish hunters, he heard something that made his skin crawl. Literally, actually, and in all ways disgustingly.

The large plant that had stopped his progress was moving. As he heard what sounded like slurping, he felt as though he was being . . . tasted. It was an altogether unpleasant sensation, much like one would feel if, Rol thought . . . well, as if one *was* being tasted. Yes, it was just like that. And it was that. And that was not at all acceptable as far as Rol was concerned. So he backed away as gracefully and tastelessly as possible until he believed he was out of reach of the plant's tentacle-tongues, though he was unable to confirm that because of the ever-present mist. When he was at last sure he was out of range, Rol gave a deep sigh of relief, took five steps to his right, and plummeted straight down the Cliffs of Largeish Heights to his immediate death on the rocks below.

Almost.

He fell surprisingly far, landing uncomfortably with the wind knocked out of him on a small muddy outcropping. Trying to stand up, he slipped in the mud, plunged over the edge of the small ledge, and continued his fall. There were no jagged rocks when he landed, and that was encouraging. But there was a swampy, muddy mess that cushioned his fall but also, unfortunately, threatened to hold him fast. He struggled to keep his head up and push-pull himself out of the mud. And he did so successfully but not without using up practically every ounce of energy. A little dazed and working his way to what he thought was a dry area, he focused on taking one single step and then another. But one step too far had him teetering precariously on the edge of another cliff and then dropping over the side, with his pack breaking loose and disappearing as he fell.

Tough situation, Rol thought with little emotion sometime later.

Do I want the bad news or the bad news first? he thought.

No pack, no food or drink. Obviously, no fifty feet of rope. Just the clothes he was wearing, which were wet and muddy, and soon would be cold.

"Colder," he muttered under his breath, which he could see puffing in the moonlight.

"But you have certainly faced tougher situations," he argued to himself.

"No. Not really. This is bad," retorted his original, less hopeful self.

That assessment left his slightly more hopeful self struggling to recall a time when the situation was worse in hopes of pointing out that instance and thereby winning the dreary argument. Unfortunately, nothing came to mind but the present predicament, in all its bad predicamentness.

Rol was stuck in the dark in a large hunting pit with smooth walls, a muddy floor, thick wooden spikes, and no way out. How did he survive the fall, anyway? It appeared he fell conveniently between the spikes—somehow. It didn't make much sense. He should have been impaled on at least one or two or three of the things, but—unbelievably—he fell between them. Somehow. But now, instead of being stuck on a spike at the bottom of a muddy pit, he was just stuck at the bottom of a muddy pit. Which he was not getting out of anytime soon.

But at least he had a chance.

A chance to dreadfully starve or freeze to death, Rol thought.

Yes, but still a chance.

So he waited for it. The starving part. It would be coming. The freezing bit, possibly sooner. A few moments and then a few more moments, it would all blend together—all the same—until none of it mattered. A small part of Rol considered that scenario as a real possibility. When it started to grow strong enough for him to actually believe it, Rol got angry. *Believe it? That's what it comes down to? Believing in the hopelessness of an end this way, and that is it? Right here, before I even get a good start on my greatest adventure so far?*

Yes, he thought. *Hope may be somewhere in the general area, but right now it is hiding successfully from me.*

Rol was hungry. He was tired. He was *hired*. Or was it *tungry*? It was silly, but he laughed anyway. Giggled ridiculously, actually. He was definitely exhausted after that chase and then the falls, and now he was down there in the pit. But where was the Torg horde? Where was he? And was *tungry* any better than *hired*?

Rol decided after a day and a half, still stuck in the pit, that none of that mattered.

CHAPTER 12

I'M ON AN ADVENTURE (AND SO AM I)

An unexpected end of a rope slapped Rol in the face. The rope was familiar. The voice saying "Grab hold!" was not.

"I found a pack and a conveniently long coil of quality rope," said the rescuer a few moments later. "Not sure how else I could have pulled you out of there. I have to admit, I wasn't smart enough to have rope—what is this, fifty feet?—with me, and this is really good stuff. I'm impressed."

"Thank you for pulling me out of that pit," said Rol. "I'm forever grateful. I could have been stuck in there for days, or longer. Not entirely fun, as you can imagine."

"More than happy to help, and I wasn't doing much of anything anyway," said the stranger, who appeared to Rol to be approximately his own age. The soon-to-be-acquaintance-but-for-now-still-a-stranger held up the rope, "I guess this must be yours," he said. "That pack over there, too. I set it up on that rock, out of the mud. Looks like you were prepared for most things, although the pit was not expected, I guess."

"No," said Rol sheepishly, "Not part of my plan at all. By the way, name is Rol, and again, I thank you." He held out his hand to shake, as a sign of: "Thank you—glad to be out of the pit. We could probably be friends, but I'm sure you have your own life to live. Good-bye. I must be on my way, and the first item on my agenda is to eat anything that I might have left in my pack that has been lying on the ground for the past two or so days."

"Kearth is my name," replied Kearth, who reached out his own hand. But instead of shaking Rol's hand, he grasped his forearm, near the inside of his elbow. Rol mimicked the traditional greeting that he had heard about but had never experienced. It was a less formal greeting, or good-bye action, and one that was not often used anymore. It was considered outdated.

Rol smiled and said, "Well, again, I thank you, Kearth, and hope that you have safe travels ahead. Should be a good day for walking, at least while the sun is out. I must be on my way. After I check my pack to see if anything is left."

"What do you mean by that?" replied Kearth, offended.

"Oh. No. I didn't mean anything about you," Rol replied, backpedaling. "What I meant was that I was inconveniently in that mud pit for almost two days, and since I didn't have my pack with me, I was imagining that every small creature in the area had found my miniscule supply of food and shared it with their friends. A regular party, I'm sure. I haven't eaten anything for quite some time, and I just wanted to check if there was anything that I could snack on."

"Hmmm. Well, in case there isn't anything left, I have a few crackly spindle-crackers I could let you have. Not much, but all I can offer at the moment," said Kearth, pulling a few from his pack and holding them out in the palm of his hand.

At the sight and sound of his favorite snack, Rol drooled. It wasn't his fault, just a natural response after not having eaten recently. He reached out and took a handful of the crackers, shoving a couple into his mouth.

"These are my favorite," munch-spoke Rol. "I started off with a few of my own, but they ran out quickly. I guess I didn't think to replenish my supply with all the walking and thinking I've been doing. The little creatures and the large plant distracted me, as did the empty tent town, and then I ended up in this lonely pit."

Again a "Hmmm" and then, "Sounds like little more than an afternoon walk. But not very much more," added

Kearth in a sarcastic tone.

"Actually, I'm on an adventure," proudly announced Rol, standing up straight and tall.

"I'm oh-so-terribly happy for you."

"That's not very nice to say."

"What? I'm serious."

"You don't sound terribly happy for me. You sound, I don't know—seriously against me or something."

"Against you? Me? I'm just saying that it doesn't sound like much of an adventure. At least not so far."

"I'm just getting started. What do you expect?"

"Some adventure maybe."

"Maybe it's about to happen."

"A real adventure? With magic and sorcery and wizards and sorcery and magic and stuff?"

"No, I don't expect anything like that. Those aren't real."

"What about magic beans or magic or sorcery or magic duck eggs?"

"No, I don't think so. And where did you hear about magic duck eggs?"

"What about a talking narwhal?"

"What? I don't know what that is—so, no."

"What about a fierce, talking narwhal-eating dragon?"

"No. Wait, do you mean the narwhal thing can talk or the dragon can talk? Never mind. No."

"What about some pebbles with just a little magic in them?"

"No. Don't expect those, either."

"Why not?"

"They aren't real. That stuff is made up. People invent those things because they think that exciting made-up creatures and abilities will take them away on a grand adventure. Away from their work or their responsibilities or the irritating itch on the back of their earlobe. You can't pretend that your real life doesn't exist but that a made-up life does exist and is better than what you have right now."

"Why not?"

Kearth rescuing Rol was an interesting start to an interesting friendship. They were from very different worlds and had very different perspectives on the world they shared. Still, there were some similarities. Both were on their own at the moment, which was one, and both were the same age, give or take a season or three, which was another. They might almost have been viewed as brothers, or maybe cousins. Distant cousins.

Kearth said that he was traveling simply to see the countryside. No real plan. Looking for something other than home, which apparently for Kearth was many days' travel away. When Rol asked about his parents, Kearth quickly changed the subject. Rol didn't press the issue. They spoke instead about Rol's plan for his own journey. Kearth listened intently and then mentioned that he could accompany Rol for awhile, as long as there would be adventure along the way—specifically, until boredom set in or they reached Rol's destination, whichever came first.

"I'm honored," said Rol.

"Traveling companions it is, then," replied Kearth, and they walked in the direction Rol decided they should be going, not able to fully rely on the map at this time after his unplanned redirection recently.

The two of them walked side by side, and Rol occasionally glanced over at his new walking companion to try to learn something from Kearth, who had been mostly quiet. Kearth had wavy light brown hair that was in his eyes much of the time. He moved in a carefree manner, although he did not smile much. As he walked, his gaze was focused on the ground a few paces in front of him, rather than taking in the broader view of the world in which he lived. Seemingly not interested. Kearth's traveling gear seemed comparable to Rol's, minus any rope. He had no weapon so far as Rol could see, although Rol's own weapon was his walking stick, which probably did not appear threatening to others.

Rol recalled a conversation he once had with DaTerrin about uncertainty and believing in others. Rol decided to trust Kearth. He understood that doing so was possibly a risk, but he had a good feeling about his new fellow journeyer. They both trod along, sometimes talking about things in general, sometimes silent. Mostly silent.

A day and a half later, more or less, Rol and Kearth entered the small village of Tisbetterhere, because that was what the sign on the outskirts said to do. It was an average-looking village, as far as the buildings and general hubbub went. It turned out that Tisbetterhere had an interesting village-wide custom, though—and one that was disconcerting to Rol and Kearth as they entered the main area.

Whenever standing around in the village—whether engaged in conversation or just idle doing-nothingness—it was customary for the villagers to strike the same pose. Each stood with the right leg straight and the right foot grounded, and the left leg bent at an angle so that the bottom of the left foot rested on the inside of the right knee and the left knee pointed straight out, as though it had some grand purpose, though it didn't seem to matter where or what it pointed straight out to. It sounds stranger than it looked, which was not all that strange until you came upon everyone in an entire village standing in such a fashion—men, women, children, leaders of the community, and the village least-intelligent-person, as well as any animal that could stand that way, which was none. The denizens of Tisbetterhere called the custom "just standlingling around." Proudly, they took great pride in the fact that, as they put it, "We are, in fact, the only ones who do this sort of thing, really."

There was, in fact, an official document stating as much. It was tucked away in a tiny but official-looking building in the middle of the village, which was nothing more than an empty room containing a table with a single drawer, no chair, meant to officially, but not in any advertised manner, contain said standlingling document.

Rol and Kearth bought supplies they needed to replenish but soon left the village. Conveniently for this story, just as it was out of their sight behind them, immediately ahead was a new collection of buildings forming something akin to a small village. Akin to a small village it was, and actually aching to be a small village, which it was frustratingly not. A hand-scrawled sign announced the hamlet of Betterthanthem. It also incorporated a crude drawing of a person standing in perfect standlingling form.

As Rol walked past the sign and into the hamlet-not-village, a large man standing in the unnatural standlingling manner yelled to him. The yelling was definitely a greeting, which was a relief to Rol, who was not accustomed to being yelled at by large men standing in a way that was—he thought the word but did not say it—*ungrownmanlylike.*

It didn't take long for greetings and handshakes to be exchanged and for the large man to complete the odd-way-of-standing story by telling Rol and Kearth how his hamlet-townette came up with the pose and that all who lived there took pride in the fact that, as he put it "We are, in fact, the only ones who do this sort of thing, really." Not wanting to contradict him, Rol and Kearth just smiled and said they had to move along.

As they were passing through the one-horse hamlet, on their way out of the minor madness that appeared to have affected the hamlet folk, Rol saw that a crowd had gathered off to one side, and he decided to investigate. All of them standlingling and murmuring in a large circle near a hastily pitched tent, the locals were gathered around someone who was talking loudly.

Taking in the murmurs, Rol gathered that the denizens of Betterthanthem called the loud man the Mighty Dragonhunter. He looked like a dragonhunter, if anyone had ever seen one, which, admittedly, no one ever had. The man had a brown-leather patch over his left eye, and his right leg was a piece of wood in the shape of a piece of wood that looked like it was trying minimally to look like a leg, with a few supposed dragon bites and scratches added for effect. He seemed to get around just fine and didn't complain, although he used his battle-scarred appearance for full effect when speaking and exaggerating a limp in front of the crowd. Apparently, he told his dragon stories wherever he went, which seemed to be everywhere.

"Best darn draggunhunter and wrastler anywhere, Yup! I can outrun, outtalk, outwit, outspit, and outbreathe any dang draggun with all of my hands tied behind my back, Yup! Don't believe me? Well, I'd show ya right here, right now, if it weren't fer my show tonight in this lovely hamlet. I would, too. 'Course there awrn't no dragguns in these parts . . . not ones worth spittin' at anyway. But if you come to ma show tonight, I'll give ya somethin' to see, Yup! One night only, I might add, and if ya're havin' a tough time findin' tickets . . . Well, now . . . I reckin' . . . since you are my new friends and all . . . I guess I could talk 'em inta knockin' down a wall and puttin' in more seats, Har! Bring yar brothers and sisters and mothers and fathers and cousins and uncles and mothers and brothers and uncles and come to ma show. I'll give ya somethin' to see, Yup!"

Moving toward the front of the crowd—which was easy to do because everyone was standlingling around in a complexly organized fashion—Rol felt compelled to challenge the man's probably improbable claims and did so by saying, "What kinds of dragons have you seen, mighty dragonhunter?"

The nonflustered dragonhunter spat on the ground. The hamlet folk shuffled back a few steps. “Bigger and nastier ones than you’ve ever imagined my fine young lad,” the dragonhunter said, punctuating the comment with another spit. More shuffling from the hamlet folk.

“And how did you escape from their magic and their flames, O spitter-in-the-face-of-dragons?”

“Come to my show and I will reveal my secrets of anti-dragon magicizing and defire-breathingness. Don’t be late, or you will miss the bonus magic items I have for sale, before the show, for a limited-time special price. And bring your uncles and cousins.” With that, he pushed through the crowd and went inside his crusty tent.

As if had been rehearsed, those in the crowd shifted collectively—each standing on his or her grounded right foot to face Rol and Kearth. Rol noticed scowls on most of their faces and thought it appropriate to leave Betterthanthem right away since he had interrupted the sales pitch from the hamlet’s supposed hero.

CHAPTER 13

I LOVE A CHALLENGE

As Rol and Kearth prepared to make their exit from Betterthanthem, they came across what appeared to be the most decrepit building among all the shops in the heart of the hamlet. The sign above the door spelled out "M-A-G-I-C-S-H-O-P-P-E," and the way it was presented, the two words appeared to be one long word. Kearth mentioned that there was also an extra *P* and *E* at the end of what should have been "S-H-O-P," and he didn't trust the sign at all. Intrigued, though, the two of them walked in and were immediately astounded.

The inside of the "shoppe" looked astonishingly more tumbledown than the outside. It was dusty, dirty, and cob-webby, but it also had a certain musty smell that was quite nice, for those who liked that sort of thing.

A very elder elder greeted them with an ungainly wave, then motioned toward the middle of the room, watching Rol and Kearth intently as they stepped farther into his sales territory. There were three long tables, each with space for various whatchamacallits on sale, all nicely labeled for the benefit of the customers:

The Wand of Wonderfully Wonderful Wonders

The Glowing Sword of Dennis the Part-time Wizard-Thief

Magic Beans of Klaus Krammerfitzen

The Serving Plate of Perpetual Destiny

Rol marveled that some two dozen items must have been showcased, each with an exotic-sounding name and each seeming to be deemed capable of some amazingly magical function. The shoppekeeper mentioned, with a slightly troubled and troubling smirk, that they were all one-of-a-kind beauties, never-before-seen in these parts, and were conveniently linked with not-to-be-passed-up special offers—for one day only.

Rol picked up the Wand of three *W*s. "What does this do?" he inquired.

"It was used by the legendary magician Spell-o, as he fought the minions of the Darkish One," the shoppekeeper replied.

"I haven't heard of any of them," challenged Rol. "When was that?"

"Many eons ago, of course. Many eons and more. I just happened to come across this beauty recently and wanted to offer it from the kindness of my own heart to the awaiting public."

"What does it do?"

"Well, that's a good question. The answer is that I haven't actually tried it. Been meaning to. Just have been busy-busy-busy these past few months, what with the opening of this new shoppe, of course. I'm sure I'll get to it one of these days."

"Look at these, Rol," said Kearth, grinning and pointing to the "magic" beans on the table. "What about these beans?" he asked the shoppekeeper. "What do they do?"

"They, in fact, don't do anything at the moment. They would do something, but I haven't quite figured out how to activate them without Klaus' Black Pot of Bean Activation. You see, Klaus passed away many years ago, and his pot has been missing since then. I have some people looking for it, but so far . . . Well, you know how it is."

"Do any of these legendary magic objects actually have

magic in them?" probed Rol.

"My friend, it is an interesting choice of words you used when saying that the magic is 'in them.' Sometimes magic can be *in* a magic item or sometimes it can come *from* a magic item. Or magic can be around it or associated with it. I don't know how that works exactly, and so I am not sure why I mentioned it—but I did and there you go."

"'Associated with magic'? What does that mean?"

"I told you, I don't know. Let's just say I never said that."

"But you haven't answered the real question. Do any of these magic items actually have magic, produce magic, or are in some way associated with magic, as you said you never said?"

Thinking hard for a moment, sweat dripping from the one brow, the shoppekeeper confidently stated, "No. No magic. Not now. But see, this one used to be able to . . ."

"But none of these work now, do they? How do you know that they ever worked magic?"

"I heard the stories, of course. And read about them in the brochures."

"And you never doubted them?"

"Well . . . no. But see, this one has a really good tale of . . ."

Rol had had enough. He left the shop—er, the *shoppe*—with Kearth following close behind, both shaking their heads unconsciously and, at the same time, consciously.

The shoppekeeper followed the two of them as far as the doorway. Noticing others in the general area, he said loudly, "Thanks for visiting! Don't forget to tell your friends about the great deals. This week only." He then looked around hopefully. Realizing that he had not attracted anyone's attention, he shrugged and meandered back to the sales floor.

Kearth and Rol left the hamlet of Betterthanthem so quickly and thoroughly that they completely forgot about the dragonhunter show that night. Later that day, Kearth mentioned that although he wished they could see the show and hear the tales, it was not worth going back. Rol joked that by the end of their journey they would have enough tales of their own to put on a show, although dragons were not likely to be associated with their stories of bravery.

"I don't think we should mention standlingling to anyone," quipped Rol, "or they may ask us to demonstrate."

The next leg of their travels led them to lands that most likely had never before been seen by more than a handful of living beings. There were rushing rivers, craggy cliffs, hill-mountains and even full-grown mountains—some that were labeled or drawn on Rol's map, some that were not. Late one morning, at the top of a mountain, Rol and Kearth stood in a chilly breeze, considering their options. They had to get from here to there. Basically, as Rol saw the challenge in front of them, they had to make their way across the deepest chasm he had ever seen, then proceed from the top of the tallest, craggiest mountaintop ever to the top of the second-tallest and even craggierest mountaintop of all mountaintops.

Apparently, the only way across was via the most rickety wood-and-rope suspension bridge ever devised, with it swinging humorlessly and precariously while dangling unpredictably with its nefariously long length and dangerously thin width just waiting to be traversed with no hope of success whatsoever. That was the first step. Then it would all get somewhat more difficult.

Rol loved a challenge. So he said to his faithful companion, "You know, Kearth, I love a challenge."

His faithful companion *did* know, because on their journey so far the map had led them through the Straits of Straight-up Pain, into the Cave of We'll Have None of That, and over the River of Aaaaaaaaaaaagh . . . Splash . . . Ohnooooo. And he had not only survived those escapades but also had the telltale scars to prove it. Kearth showed off those scars as much as possible to everyone he met to prove how willing he was to face a challenge, even though he had not actually initiated any challenge, but he still bragged as though he did.

So he said to Rol in reply, "Oh. OK then."

Which is exactly what one says when they unbravely realize they don't have a choice in the matter and they will have to go along anyway, which will mean some good scars or at least a slight twitch from the ordeal.

Rol and Kearth crossed the bridge without incident. It was about as unexciting to Kearth as the time he fell asleep while lying on his back, listening to the wings of butterflies fluttering in a meadow's breeze as he watched the billowy clouds pass overhead. Which was fine with him.

Several days later, standing at the top of a small mountain, Rol and Kearth could see the wonder of the lands all around them. The leaves on the trees had recently changed to bright oranges, deep purples, and striking reds. The sun was shining on a lazy river winding its way through a forest and open fields, with glints of light reflecting in the ripples as the water rolled over rocks and logs caught in the flow. A light wind shifted trees one way or another, passing through with just enough force to carry away a leaf now and then.

Even the rocks beneath their feet seemed magnificent, as though Rol were seeing rocks for the first time in his life. Some were rounded, others sharp and angled, others flat and unevenly shaped, but all seemed to be just the way that they were meant to be.

It was a good day.

Kearth was complaining about something or other but less strenuously than usual—and even that enhanced the overall goodness.

Wanting to stand there on the mountaintop forever, Rol expressed that thought to Kearth, who did not say anything but made his reply known by lifting his head to the breeze, closing his eyes, and smiling. Rol and Kearth stood in the welcoming sun, and then surveyed what lay ahead for them. From their perch, they understood they had to find a way down the small mountain, through a lush valley, and then up the side of the mountain range directly across from them. If they moved at a reasonable pace and did not stop, they could summit the other mountain before dark. It appeared that would be a good place for them to stop for the night. The vantage point would make it possible for them to look back into the valley as a precautionary measure for protection in the dark while also maybe affording a view of whatever awaited them beyond the next mountain, which they would encounter the following day. It was a good plan, a sound plan—and probably an unrealistic plan, based on what Rol had just happened to notice.

Down in the lush valley, possibly a hundred paces from the flowing river, was a house they had failed to notice just moments before. The stone-and-wood walls were camouflaged by the surrounding trees and moss that grew on the semi-flat surfaces of the structure. There was a small path leading to what was maybe a front door—from the distance, it was hard to be sure. It was a wisp of smoke coming from the chimney on the side of the abode nearest to Rol and Kearth that gave away its location. Rol imagined the owner to be a brave soul, as the house appeared to be the only structure in the entire valley, and although that meant quite a bit of elbow room for the inhabitant, it also meant being open to attack from anyone or anything that might be looking for easy prey.

Their shared mood slightly changed, Rol and Kearth started down the mountainside, both glancing around to keep a sharp eye on their surroundings. It was ridiculous to think that all of a sudden there would be an attack just because they had arrived on the scene, but it was best not to take any chances. Cautiously, they made their way down the mountain, looking for any sign of life near the house—or of someone watching Rol and Kearth as they approached what was obviously not their property.

At the edge of a clearing no more than fifty paces from the house, Rol and Kearth stopped to look around, listen carefully, and even smell the air for signs of life—whether good or bad. They were standing in tall weeds they believed would keep them hidden, and they were confident they had made all the right moves as they approached the house. Kearth wanted to yell out their intentions so as not to surprise anyone who might not have expected or approved of visitors who happened to happen by. Rol was about to say that was probably a good idea when they suddenly heard a voice call out—not from the direction in front of them, which they expected, but instead from directly behind them, which they did not.

CHAPTER 14

FLOWING TEARS AND NOISY NOSES

"It appears that I have guests. I was not expecting guests. I'm not sure these are guests at all. Maybe they are here to be more than guests. Maybe they are here to steal my dunfapples, eh?"

Rol turned around without any sudden movements. The man who stood in front of him and Kearth looked pleasant enough, except for the long and extremely sharp farm tool he pointed threateningly at them.

Rol quickly told their story. The man was more than pleasant, and it didn't take much convincing for him to lower his tool-turned-temporary-weapon and invite Kearth and Rol into his house. Between bites of bread and slurps of gravy that he shared with the two visitors, he told them that he was a farmer, tending an orchard of golden dunfapples, which his guests had never seen before. In addition to growing dunfapples, he got along by catching fish from the river, which were plentiful. The farmer did not hunt, so he had no meat to eat or furs to keep him warm. He lived alone and was happy with his life, rarely seeing anyone else, which was suitable for him. It was good at this time, though, for him to have others to talk to—and for Rol and Kearth to have another person in the mix—and Rol and Kearth stayed the night. The trio talked most of the night, telling tall tales and a few that were true, mostly. In the morning they parted ways, but not before the farmer gave his visitors dunfapples for their journey—as many as they cared to carry.

That night, after a full day of walking, Rol and Kearth happened upon a camp with a blazingly bright fire. Wandering carefully into the area, but not cautiously enough, they were greeted by fifteen warriors—male and female—who were not as hospitable as their farmer host had been. Rol and Kearth were immediately captured and tied up to a nearby tree with straps made from animal hide. They tried to explain their situation but were ignored. The warriors dug through their packs, separating the edibles into piles off to one side. Rol noticed that Kearth had a small stash of crackly spindle-crackers that he had not mentioned at all. Rol drooled instinctively. Other food was piled up, including the dunfapples, which garnered much attention.

"What are thems and where you get?" angrily questioned the apparent leader of the small tribe, who had wavy red-brown hair and a full beard to match, though the latter was clumped with spilled food and not quite as red as it should have been. In fact, it looked a little more . . . moldy green.

"Dunfapples," Rol responded faux-knowingly, as he had been introduced to them only the day prior. He added, "We found them," as he did not want any harm to come to the gracious farmer.

"Show me tomorrow day where you found, and you live, if I in good," said the leader. Rol, mentally filling in the last word, believed that a good *mood* was most likely not in the leader's future.

It was convenient that the lead warrior spoke roughly the same language as Rol and Kearth—otherwise their adventure might have come to an unpleasant and abrupt end right there and then. The leader's use of language was definitely interesting, and took some straining to understand. Rol glared at Kearth, trying with his eyes to impart the importance of not making any comments about the butchered language.

The two captives were left where they were, strapped to a tree all night, although able to sit with their legs out in front of them, while the others slept by the warm fire. Only one captor was "volunteered" to stand guard. The warriors were confident they could all have a nice snooze while one from their ranks would handle any situation that went awry during the night with the weakling prisoners, which they believed was not a likely scenario, although they didn't use any of those exact words, except for *nice* and *snooze*.

Unable to do anything at the moment, Kearth slept soundly, snoring rhythmically along with the fierce warriors, as if the cacophony had been rehearsed. The situation did not look good to Rol, and he did not sleep. Instead, his mind wandered. He was angry.

He was angry at the situation, and at his parents, and at DaTerrin. Whether his master was alive or not—Rol went back and forth in his mind with different theories about that—Rol felt abandoned, and even betrayed. Reflecting on his uncle's departure, it almost seemed to have been purposefully arranged. DaTerrin mentioned Mapinashu on a couple of occasions, obviously as a clue, and there was that time he had mysteriously set off to meet with the town leaders. What did that mean? Was there anything about that meeting that Rol might have missed? Over and over, the thoughts tumbled through Rol's mind, building to the point that he was shaking in frustration. Why was he abandoned? How could they do that to him?

Without warning, a different thought crept into Rol's mind. One that he had successfully locked away for the many days since DaTerrin was taken. Rol remembered that he had delayed their departure from the top of the hill-mountain, which meant they had to try to make their way home after the sun went down and the day's light was lost. The grumblegoblins had taken Rol's master in the dark, which would not have happened had they left sooner. It was Rol's fault. It was Rol's fault that his uncle was taken. It was Rol's selfishness that caused his uncle's capture and presumed death.

Guilt was the most difficult emotion for Rol to experience. Loss was bad enough, but causing that loss was beyond anything he had imagined. His tears flowed freely and the shaking worsened, threatening to wake someone up, although probably not Kearth, the slumber wonder.

It was all so confusing, and Rol was more frustrated than ever. He had not expressed his feelings about this matter to Kearth, but they had been there, hidden from all, even his inner self, until just then. Rol generally acted joyful and fine with all situations—and he tried to be in a good frame of mind each day—but it was terribly hard for him to feel that way in his own heart.

The tears continued. The night went on and passed Rol by.

The next morning, Kearth and an emotionally exhausted Rol started walking with pointy spears at their backs. Rol didn't want to lead the warriors to the farmer, but he also knew that they must produce some fruit, or a bad mood was bound to find the warrior leader. Along the way back to the farm, Rol tried to strike up a conversation, hoping that doing so would somehow help him formulate a plan for getting out of the mess. Reluctant in the beginning, the tribal leader didn't take long to open up.

"We Eye Lenders. Fierce tribe. Scary we. Great and scary me most," said the leader, among other nonsensical things.

Rol, trying to play to the leader's sense of self-importance, said, "Oh, great Eye Lender leader. You are much scary." He went on about how scary he was, and then how much greater he would be if he were to help someone in need while getting something useful in return. It was a long conversation, as Rol had to speak slowly while also trying to understand what was inferred by "Me scary and brave Eye Lender" and other oft-repeated words and phrases that were difficult to decipher.

In the end, Rol won him over. As they walked and talked, they were moving toward the farmer's cottage, and eventually they arrived. Upon being released, Rol went inside to make arrangements with the farmer, taking along the tribe's leader. It took the better part of the day, but in the end, they had finalized a trade agreement by which the farmer would provide dunfapples and fish in exchange for meat and furs from the Eye Lenders. That agreement would continue whenever the warriors were in the area. For the first exchange, it also extended to items including three long ropes and a backpack of various bread items from the farmer in exchange for a nifty snakeskin headband from the warrior leader.

Rol and Kearth parted ways with the farmer and the warriors to journey on, having had a good lesson in diplomacy. They had also learned a lesson in what it might take to win certain people over. While Rol was busy with the trade agreement, Kearth had waited outside. He did not do well with situations in which making concessions and talking calmly were necessary. Not having a role in the talks, and standing directly in front of a dozen or so of the fierce warriors, Kearth was at a loss as to what he should do next.

His mind took him back to a similar situation he had experienced as a younger. He was confronted by a gang of older youngers who wanted to teach him a lesson about who was boss, and who was not. Not knowing what to do, Kearth suggested loudly that he would harshly do *this* and *that* and another *this* and one more *that* to them—demonstrating what would happen by cupping his hands over his nose and making a cracking sound by clicking his thumbnails under his front teeth—without the boys seeing the thumb motion, of course, which made them think he was actually painfully cracking his nose. They were taken by surprise, and to Kearth's relief, laughter came instead of an attack. It was a successful diversion tactic that Kearth had used on later occasions.

He tried that ploy in front of the Eye Lenders, which in a similar manner resulted in surprised smiles, laughter, and the words "show how" from the tribesmen. Despite the warriors' terribly gnarled thumbnails with nasty gunk embedded beneath, Kearth's demonstration and instruction were thoroughly successful. The result was a ceaseless cacophony of clicking sounds and fake nose-cracking movements, which triggered thunderous laughter. The act was repeated again and again—interrupted only by excited waves goodbye—until Kearth and Rol were out of sight and earshot.

The duo quickly journeyed on to put some distance between themselves and the tribe, just in case there was a change of heart or the nose-cracking hilarity wore off. They filled the next two days by recounting the adventures of the previous two days, and they realized that quick thinking beat a sharp spear point. At least that time it did.

More days of walking followed, without much excitement.

"To pass the time, we can play a game," said Rol, having grown tired of walking, one morning.

"Sounds fun. At least more fun than just walking. What kind of game?" said Kearth, who was also over the whole walking thing.

"There is a game I played as a much younger," Rol explained. "It was great fun and truly didn't take any talent at all to play."

"OK then, what is this no-talent-needed, fun game of yours called?"

"Well . . . actually . . . come to think of it, you're probably not going to like it. So really, never mind. Forget I mentioned it. Say, did you see the stars last night? They were quite a sight . . ."

"Wait. No. That's enough. What about the game you mentioned? Stop changing the subject. You started with the game, then you stopped. Now I demand you start again! What is the game called and why are you hesitating now? I demand the name! Do you understand that I am not asking now, I am demanding! Demanding, I tell you!" Kearth spouted, stomping his foot with every exclamation.

"That is somewhat obvious. Listen, why don't you just calm down and we can move on to something else? What's for lunch anyway?"

"No! There will be no lunch and no more changing the subject until you tell me the name of the game, and then, after that, there will still be no changing the subject. But then possibly lunch. I am getting a tad bit hungry, now that you mention lunch."

"Lunch is a great idea. I'm glad you mentioned it, because, well, the ol' tummer is making some pretty growly noises and all that. I wholeheartedly agree that we should start lunch and continue our discussion at another time."

"What discussion is that?"

"Look," interjected Rol, "there's a town up ahead. I bet we can have lunch there." And so there was, and so they did.

Walking into the town, they passed by a number of locals who looked at them strangely. Twice, Rol heard someone say, ". . . just like that other one," and then hurry off. It was disconcerting. Rol and Kearth agreed to leave as soon as they had lunch and bought supplies for the next leg of the journey. Uneasy about the situation, they would not stay the night, even though they were each looking forward to a comfortable bed.

They found a local eating establishment and wandered in through the open door of The Battering Ram. It was a little early for lunch, but because they were not going to stay in town long, this was their only opportunity. Besides, they figured the service would be at its best since there would be few customers.

Rol and Kearth sat down at a table and ordered the special, since it was the only option, which made the idea of it being "special" truly contradictory. The owner of the pub seemed nervous about their presence, and he worked hard to keep them happy, no doubt in hopes of hurrying them along soon. Rol and Kearth made small talk. Rol explained that the idea of the word game they were playing prior to reaching the town was to start a conversation and then completely, and successfully, change the subject. Kearth didn't get it. Rol tried his explanation again, but Kearth didn't see the point in it. Rol agreed that there was no real, intellectually suitable point to the game, but what, he asked, could be expected from youngers who also played "I Spy With My Good Eye . . . ?"

Finally, their food was brought to them on large, warm platters. A heaping portion of battered and fried mutton with a side of fresh vegetables. Digging in with gusto, Kearth and Rol stopped talking and just ate, savoring every bite, every bit.

Only moments into their meal, they noticed a dark figure who entered through the open door and, stopping briefly to look around, walked directly to the travelers' table and sat down on the vacant wooden chair next to them.

"I heard the townsfolk talking about you, and I came to see for myself," the stranger said. "Nice traveling hat," he directed at Rol.

Looking up but still chewing, Rol and Kearth continued

chewing.

“We can talk when you’ve finished,” the new arrival said, then added loudly to the pub owner, “Bring me a drink. Water is fine—clean this time. And if I see a slice of lemon in it, you will be wearing it permanently—the lemon, not the water. Also, a plate of what they’re having.”

Rol continued to eat and was about to speak, but first had more swallowing to do. Kearth didn’t even think about talking, which would have interrupted his meal.

“Don’t let me stop you,” said the new almost-acquaintance, “I will talk. You will listen. By all means, continue chewing. It looks as though you need the nourishment.”

CHAPTER 15

TAGGING ALONG

"My name is Fhfyrd," explained Fhfyrd, pronouncing it "Feared" in a normal manner and then again in a much slower and more deliberate way. "*Fhfyrd.* It's easy to remember and difficult to forget. It says about all that needs to be said about me. I'm Fhfyrd. Feared. Fhfyrd wherever I go. Do I make myself clear? And the *Fh* is silent. Got a problem with that?"

Rol and Kearth both nodded and then shook their heads, still chewing.

Fhfyrd's mutton not-so-special special came, and he started eating while Rol took in the sight of him. The younger was probably a few seasons older than both Kearth and Rol—hard to be sure with all the dirt and the slight, almost a whisper, of whiskers on his jaw. Dressed in black from head to toe. Rugged, haggard, jagged, ragged. Probably possessed slight intelligence, definitely exhibited more than slight attitude, and presented well the "outdoors type" of look—most likely with the skill and experience to back it up. He had a scabbard with a long sword hanging from his waist, and the pack on his back had something resembling a large wooden horseshoe tied to it.

"Word is, you're looking for a traveling companion," said Fhfyrd knowingly although wrongly.

His plate clean, Rol could at last speak. "No. Not us. We're just passing through, actually."

Kearth, wiping gravy from his lips with the back of his hand, added, "And if we were, we would not be looking for you."

Fhfyrd put his half-chewed food down on his plate. Not what was already in his mouth, of course. That would be gross. He then wiped his entire black-sleeved arm across his mouth and sat back in his chair, staring at Kearth. A mighty laugh came from deep down inside him, and then he drew in a long breath, which made Rol nervous because he feared Fhfyrd was choking. Another laugh put Rol's fears to rest, and Rol wiped his arm across his forehead, removing the embarrassing sweat that had beaded up in the tense situation.

Speaking with controlled inflection, Rol said, "I'm Rol

and this is Kearth. As I said, you must be looking for someone else. We are traveling, yes, but in no need of anyone else tagging along."

A half-laughing Fhfyrd said, "Tagging along, is it? Well, I think I could be of more value than that. Anyway, I think these lovely townsfolk would be as pleased as a skrat in a dung pile if we were to leave their lovely village as soon as possible. Isn't that right, Mr. Pub Owner?" That last remark was loud enough to be heard by absolutely everyone in the pub—that being just the three of them and the owner. Addressing Rol, Fhfyrd then said, "I heard you came from the west, and that most likely means you are heading east, unless I'm mistaken, and I'm sure I'm not. I happen to be going that way myself. I could use someone new to talk to, although I'm actually pretty good company, if I do say so myself, which I do. But if you're anything like me, and I know *I* am, then a different voice and a fresh set of adventure stories make the journey less monotonous."

Kearth was impressed that Fhfyrd even knew the word *monotonous* and said so under his breath.

Fhfyrd laughed again and reached into his money pouch. He produced enough coins to pay for the food eaten by the three of them and flipped them onto the table, saying a raucous thank-you to the pub owner. Then he stood up and headed toward the door, inviting Rol and Kearth to follow him. Outside, where the light was better, Rol could see scars on the face and hands of their new friend. He also was able to identify the item on Fhfyrd's pack as a rarely seen musical instrument.

Fhfyrd bowed slightly and spoke in an eloquent manner, saying, "Fhfyrd of the Black Mountains, at your service if you accept. Just me, my sword, my skill, and my trustworthy lyre."

Rol replied half kiddingly, "Trustworthy lyre? That doesn't make any sense."

They walked to an area of town Fhfyrd said he had seen earlier. Apparently, there was a shop that had something he needed for the journey. He went inside and left Rol and Kearth outside, readying their packs and discussing Fhfyrd.

"If he goes, I can't continue on with you, Rol," said Kearth.

"Why?" Rol questioned, perplexed.

"We don't know anything about him, and my mother always said to stay away from no good thieves and lyres."

"She said 'no good thieves and *liars*,' I'm sure."

"That's what I said."

"You said *lyres*, but I am saying *liars*."

"You're saying *liars*."

"I'm saying *liars* and *lyres*."

"You're saying *liars* and *liars*."

"No, obviously I am saying *liars* and *lyres*."

"It looks different in print but is the same when you say it."

"What do you mean it looks different in print?"

"Never mind."

"Anyway, you really can't tell the difference between *liars* and *lyres*?"

"Of course I can. Not really. No."

"Really? No?"

"No. Anyway, how do you know?"

"Know what?"

"What my mother said."

"I'm sure your mother would not want you to stay away from musical instruments."

"How do you know that?"

"What kind of mother would tell her son to stay away from musical instruments?"

"A mother who is concerned for her son. Me."

"Why would your mother be afraid of musical instruments?"

"Let's just say there was an incident and leave it at that."

"But . . ."

"Please. It's painful enough."

Just then, Fhfyrd exited the store. He had bought a nice longbow and a quiver full of arrows. All black, of course. Holding up the bow for the two potential traveling companions to admire, he said, "Shall we go?"

Kearth looked down at his feet, kicking the dust. He looked up at Rol and then at Fhfyrd. Then he looked around at nothing in particular. "Let's go," he said, putting on a brave face. The three of them headed out of the town.

Twelve days later, Kearth woke up on the cold, hard ground, looked around, and grumbled. This was not stomach rumbling in which noise comes involuntarily from somewhere inside, signaling hunger or even punishment for a night of overdoing food, drink, or . . . basically that's it—food or drink. No, this was a completely voluntary grumble, on the verge of being a full grunty complaint. A noise that sounded much like an arboar rooting in the ground for spring grubs but with indecipherable words mixed in for bad measure. Indecipherable words that arboars are not prone to using, and most likely would not choose to use even if they had the ability, which they don't. These were indecipherably intelligent-being words that often resulted in doing no good other than providing an outlet for the so-called intelligent being to voice a feeling of discomfort or an attitude of ungratefulness.

Uncomfortable and ungrateful basically described what Kearth was feeling. He was not happy about the situation and wanted everyone to know it. Not in a mean way but in a "If I am now awake and feeling miserable, then it's only fair that you share a little in my discomfort and unjoy" manner.

Surprisingly, Kearth alone was suffering foul sentiments. The other now-awake travelers in the traveling trio were, like him, still in the makeshift camp—but they did not share his grump.

"What an amazing sunrise!" proclaimed Rol, stretching his weary but nonetheless grateful arms up toward the sky, "It brings the promise of a good day of traveling and weather that will surely be on our side today. Is anyone ready for breakfast?"

"Breakfast, yes," answered Fhfyrd, his eyes still closed. "I am most definitely ready for lightly toasted mutton chunks, a large bowl of steamingly warm apple mush, and a heaping helping of potatoberry bits soaked in gravy from the aforementioned mutton. If we have any of that, that is. Otherwise, I'll grab some hunks of days-old bread from my pack. Anyone?"

Kearth stood, dumbfounded. He was trying to look "dumbfounded with a hint of dismay," but he didn't quite pull it off. Another grunt came out of him, and then a few decipherable words this time.

"Cold. Not enough sleep. Ground was hard. There's frost on me. On ME!" Kearth followed up with more complaining under his breath, which could be seen plainly because of the chilly, moist morning air. Rol clapped him heartily on the back before reaching for a hunk of the crusty bread Fhfyrd was holding out to them.

The next morning proved to be different from the start of the previous day. Kearth awoke to see Rol walking a few footsteps away from the camp they had set up. He watched as Rol stopped, knelt down, and closed his eyes. After a few minutes, Fhfyrd woke up, too. He stretched, saying, "What have you fine lads cooked up for breakfast?"

Kearth gave him a "Shhhhh" and pointed to Rol.

"What's he doing?" questioned Fhfyrd.

"Looks like he's praying," responded Kearth rather loudly, ignoring his own "Shhhhh" and then adding, "I saw someone do that a few months ago. You're supposed to be quiet, so as not to interrupt."

"Yes!" said Rol, opening one eye and half yelling. "The idea is to be respectful when someone is praying so that they can maintain focus. Common courtesy, you know."

"Sorry," said Kearth and Fhfyrd at the same time, their heads bowed in embarrassment.

A few minutes later, Rol stood up and walked over to them, packing up his things for the day's walk.

"No hard feelings," he said. "Praying is something my uncle taught me. I'm not very good at it, but I think that each time I do it I get better. Actually, I know I do. You both ought to try it sometime." Then he recounted the time DaTerrin taught him how to pray correctly, up on the hill-mountain, the day his uncle was taken away. Even though the memory brought sadness, Rol was happy to share it with Kearth and Fhfyrd. Somehow doing so helped him through the heavy bleakness he had been feeling tucked inside recently.

Observing his attitude, Fhfyrd said, "Rol, why are you always in a good mood? Or at least you never seem to be in a *bad* mood. Mostly."

Rol paused, gathered his thoughts, and replied, "I'm definitely not always in a good mood. I think about my uncle and sometimes feel angry and sad—although I guess I might not show it as much as I feel it. As far as seeming to be in a good mood all the time . . . I know that right now we are getting low on food, right? We're at the we-need-to-find-food-soon-or-we-won't-be-eating-anything-tomorrow stage, and we are barely eating as it is. But I find myself thinking: *I can be hungry and happy, or I can be hungry and in a really bad mood about it.* Either way, I'm hungry—that isn't changing. Of course, I'm not happy about being hungry, but I'm trying not to let it bring me down. It doesn't necessarily come easy, but it all ultimately comes down to choice. Most of the time I choose to be happy, and I guess that I am. Mostly."

Hearing but not really listening to Rol, Kearth said,

"That's easy for you to say, Mr. Cheery. You're happy all the time."

"Isn't that what I just . . ." started Rol, who was interrupted by a large flying object passing in front of them.

"What is that?" said Kearth.

"What? What that?" replied Rol.

"Is that a bird? No, wait—it's a moth! A huge moth! Look at that thing!"

"You're right, that is a moth. That thing is gigantic."

"It's huge!"

"It's more than that, it's giant. A giant moth. A behemoth!"

"What's that? *Behemoth*?"

"A behemoth is something huge and large, and in this case, since it is actually a moth, behe*moth* is fitting, if I do say myself."

"OK, then tell us, do you think we can eat it?"

"I don't think we would want to, no. But at least it gives me hope that there is life around here. Maybe something else lives around here that is edible. Like a squirrel. That would do."

"I'd take a behesquirrel right about now," Fhfyrd interjected. "Or even a beheweasel."

Rol recognized Fhfyrd's "hungry voice."

"Let's keep walking," he said. "There's bound to be

something we can eat just up ahead."

And coincidentally, there was. Just a few paces away, the three travelers came to some trees that had pink-red fruit growing on them. None of them knew the name of the fruit or the trees, but Fhfyrd confirmed the edibility of the fruit by grabbing one from the nearest tree, squeezing it—which was the surest way to ensure the ripeness of fruit—and biting into it.

"Midmidmeallymood," he said with a mouthful of fruit. Taking that proclamation to mean it wasn't poison, Kearth and Rol each tried his own, and both enjoyed the sweet flavor.

That evening, after a surprisingly enjoyable day of walking, Rol built a fire using some twigs, branches, and a couple of herdycones he found nearby. It sprang up quickly and soon was burning contently. The trio talked about how nice the warm glow of the fire was and the warmth it provided on such a dampish night, then grew silent, sinking deeply into their own thoughts. After what seemed to be many moments—although it was difficult to tell because time can play tricks on those lost in thought and *moments* is such a generic term—Fhfyrd spoke up.

"Rol, do you ever worry about what will happen to you?" he asked. "You know, when faced with something like you and Kearth went through recently, from all those stories you two have been telling me nonstop about these past few days having to do with a Cave of Something or other and the River of . . . I don't know, you made some weird noises. Do you ever think that could happen again, and what you might do the second time around?"

Rol, unpleasantly interrupted from pleasant thoughts about his more-often-than-not-pleasant childhood and the small murphhht he had as a pet, murmured, "There you go, boy, a nice bowl of curds for you. That's a good murphhht. Good boy."

Not nonplussed in the slightest, Fhfyrd replied, "That's not exactly the response I expected but OK, let's go with that. What's a murphhht?"

Rol replied, "It's a small, wispfully furry six-legged type of wild, yet tamable, rodent with two tails and . . . never mind . . . What I meant to say was that I don't worry about things like that. I try to prepare for them ahead of time and learn from past experiences, but I don't worry. It's a waste of time to think much about bad things that may never come to pass. You can spend a lot of time worrying and fretting, and even imagining yourself in a situation that may never come to be. I try to avoid that as much as possible."

"Interesting," Fhfyrd said. "You say that as though you're repeating what someone told you. I'm not convinced you feel that way. How can someone avoid worrying?"

Kearth jumped in with, "Wait. So what you are saying is that a murphhht is tamable? I thought they were just wild, six legs and all, and would run away at the first opportunity. That changes everything. Let's get one. We can tame it and it can perch on my shoulder as we travel and . . ."

Fhfyrd jumped in, too, with, "Didn't you hear anything Rol said? He was giving us insight into his thoughts on worrying and wasting time and other things besides just some strange rodent-thing that you want sitting on your shoulder."

"Perching, not sitting. There's a difference. I could feed it crackers and teach it to growl on command. Maybe even fetch me ale."

"You don't even drink ale."

"Well, water, then."

"Where are you going to get well water?"

"Not well water, you splint, I said "well" then "water," and they were obviously separated by a comma."

"OK, then, but what's a comma? And stop calling me splint. I don't even know what that means."

"Obviously, comma, it means someone who doesn't know their punctuation."

"But what about the perching rodent?"

The next morning, Kearth and Fhfyrd awoke to again see

Rol on his knees, eyes closed, silent. They were quiet until he finished, recognizing Rol's position of prayer they had seen the day prior.

After eating their morning meal, all three of them slowly packed up, not anxious to be on the move again. Wandering around the camp they had set up the night before, Rol soon happened upon a stream. The water rushing over the rocks relaxed him, and he lost himself in the small sounds and continuous flow. He eyed a fairly large rock that looked comfortable enough to sit on, and he did just that. Boots off, feet in the cool water. He was soon joined by his fellow journeyers.

Rol began lifting small rocks to peer beneath, hoping to see a creature living under them. He remembered fondly the many times he would play near a stream and deftly catch small creatures that lived in the water world. Colorful water lizards, with wing-shaped legs that helped them travel by using the water flow as a slight push. Blanderflits, whose pincers could deliver a tiny though painful squeeze. Snake-like fuds, which were impossible to catch unless you could coax them into your open palm with a bit of dried meat, and then you had to have lightning-fast reflexes to keep them from squirming between your fingers and escaping.

Rol shared the good memories with Kearth and Fhfyrd. They all splashed about in the stream and showed each other the interesting creatures they were able to find when they weren't muddying the water with their commotion.

It was a nice respite from the day-to-day, and was welcomed wholeheartedly. Enjoying a breath of fresh air was more important for the travelers than they could have possibly imagined as they approached the day and night ahead.

CHAPTER 16

WARTY AND MELODRAMATIC

The remainder of the day was optimal for travel, especially after the fun and stress-free morning. Rol, Kearth, and Fhfyrd walked on through open plains toward what were labeled on the map as *Breathtaking Mountains*, with *Breathtaking* underlined twice.

"I wonder what that means," wondered Fhfyrd suspiciously when he had first noticed the name on the map a few days before. Rol wasn't suspicious but kept the map tucked inside his belt for easy retrieval since Fhfyrd seemed so concerned and wanted to review the map frequently.

As the three of them approached the mountains, it was obvious that they would be crossing them, not going around. They didn't look particularly breathtaking from far away, or even close up, so they decided that the name meant there must be incredible views, somewhere in the mountain range, at least according to someone who had obviously been there at some time.

"Unless it is just a legend, a name passed down through the ages, and the connection to the name has long been forgotten," pondered Fhfyrd, who was really into the there-must-be-a-strong-connection-between-the-name-of-a-landmark-on-a-map-or-why-would-it-be-named-that point of view. Although in this case he was not yet seeing the connection, it was obviously working its way through his mind.

Eventually, they dropped their packs on the rocky ground near the top of one of the small mountains. It appeared to be a good place to set up camp for the night. After eating a decent meal of some oversized weasel creature that Fhfyrd was able to procure for them and subsequently cook over a nice fire, they leaned up against some large logs nearby. Gazing into the fire, they replayed the recent days, and a few other times thrown in for good measure.

"This place reminds me of a story I heard once, when I was much younger," said Fhfyrd, who was the only one speaking much that day. "It involved a prince and princess. I think. Yes, it was a prince, for sure, and I believe a princess, who was not related at all but from a different kingdom. Did

I mention this took place in a kingdom? And I remember now that she was not a princess."

"Just get on with it," grumbled Kearth.

"It was a kingdom in which the prince ruled," Fhfyrd continued. "And he was looking for a bride, so young women were carted in from all around to see if they measured up to said prince's standards. Of course, they were all too tall or too short. Too young or too old. Too ugly or warty or clumsy or mean, misshapen, loud, quiet, argumentative, boring, overbearing, meek—did I mention warty?"

"Yes, at least once."

". . . or snooty, frail, hairy, cagey, swindling, superfluous, treacherous, disingenuous, duplicitous, insidious, imposturous, two-faced, two-timing . . ."

"Cagey? OK, we get the idea. Can you just continue?" said Kearth who was beyond losing his patience with this Once-Upon-a-Time story.

". . . melodramatic, sycophantic, or left-handed. And so none of them fit the ideal that the prince sought. Until this one young girl arrived at the palace trying to get out of the rain—I did mention it was raining . . . or hailing, right?—and she was the one. They couldn't get married in the normal way because he was royalty and she was not—about as *not* as not could get—so they ran away, which was not the proper way to handle things, by the way, I think we all know that. So they fled from the castle and ran and ran—I don't know why they didn't have horses, because you would think with him being a prince and all . . ."

"Are you quite finished? My yawn is stuck open," Kearth groaned.

"Anyway . . . they found themselves at the top of a mountain like this one. There was a chasm that prevented them from going any farther, but conveniently there was also a large log just sitting there to help climbers get across to the other side. Of course, it probably wasn't the brightest idea, but they decided to cross the chasm—holding hands, step by step."

"Don't tell me."

"Teetering on the large log, they plumed to the icy river below. Somehow the story continued with them floating back to the castle and working out a proper courtship and wedding, but I forget the rest," concluded Fhfyrd.

"Plummeted," said Kearth, a little louder than just under his breath but not loud enough, or in such a tone, to be challenging.

"What was that?" said Fhfyrd, acting as if he had been interrupted even though his story had ended.

"Oh, nothing really. I was just mentioning that the word is *plummeted* and not *plumed*—that's all."

"I think you are wrong there, my fine traveling companion. It's *plumed*, and that's just what they did."

"*Plummeted* is what would happen by falling off a log spanning a chasm, not *plumed. Plumed* is . . . something else. But not falling from a cliff. It's *plummeted*."

"It is not. Absolutely not. Rol, tell him," concluded Fhfyrd.

But Rol was looking off in the distance, considering a few stories of his own and not caring about arguing over a word that didn't matter much. Kearth and Fhfyrd continued the exchange for a bit, back and forth, until the urge to argue just died down. The sounds of night filled the air—the breeze in the nearby trees, the insects starting their nightly songs, the far-off howl of some more than likely ferocious beast. They sat and listened.

Abruptly, Fhfyrd stood up and motioned for the others to quietly follow him. The moon was hidden behind clouds, so they walked mostly through darkness down the side of the mountain to about the halfway point. They looked back up at their camp and saw a small but blazing brightly fire that indicated where their belongings were. Fhfyrd commented on how clearly their fire stood out in the dark, noting that it could be dangerous, in certain parts, to give away their position in such a manner, in case someone or something was looking for . . .

"Food." Fhfyrd said. "There, I said it. Food. Us.

Something, some*thing* mind you, may be looking for food, and that would be one or all of us. OK, so I said it. Now we need to be careful. Sorry that you won't be able to sleep much tonight. Sorry." He mumbled something about knowing the not sleeping bit from experience as they started hiking back to camp.

As they approached the camp, Rol mentioned that they had also left their packs unguarded—and coincidentally, they soon heard noises coming from the camp. They rushed ahead to find . . .

Everything was as they had left it. The noises were merely the crackling of the fire. Fhfyrd extinguished the flames. They needed the sleep, as the next day promised to be cold and damp, which was going to make walking through the mostly open prairie difficult and tiring.

But their sleep didn't last long. Fhfyrd woke up in a state of panic. He had been dreaming peacefully about eating mutton bits as a young child, in sunshine, surrounded by family and friends. The dreamy serenity quickly turned to distress as he found himself smothered by an unnaturally large piece of mutton that he had selfishly grabbed for himself and tried to eat in one bite. Upon waking, he realized that he was not in sunshine but in semi-darkness, although not able to breathe, just as he had dreamt. Hands held up to his throat, he noticed Rol and Kearth in the same position, distraught and confused. Nothing was impeding his breathing, that he could see, but something was sapping the life from him, slowly.

Fhfyrd was on the verge of sleeping again, this time forever, and he struggled to understand what was happening. They had been sleeping; it was damp; they were on the mountaintop . . . Suddenly, he had an idea and sped over to grab Rol by the elbow. He tugged and motioned for him to follow. Wild-eyed, Kearth also followed as they moved quickly down the mountain, leaving their packs behind.

Moving down the mountain toward the valley ahead, they felt air returning to their throats and lungs, although their lungs were now burning from the hurried pace. At a point not completely on the valley floor, they stopped to catch their breath, which at least showed signs of returning.

"What . . . happened . . . up . . . there?" gasp-questioned Kearth.

"Breathtaking . . . Mountains . . ." answered Fhfyrd, massaging his throat. The three sat down on the ground, heavily. Not understanding how it could have happened, but at least still alive and able to discuss the possibilities, they checked the map for their location. There were no clues other than the label *Breathtaking Mountains* next to the rough drawing of mountains. And, Fhfyrd observed irately, the very tiny skull and crossbones that previously had gone unnoticed.

After a few moments during which Rol and Fhfyrd discussed which of them had the endurance to retrieve the packs once the sun came up, Rol gave in to Fhfyrd's perseverance. Kearth watched Fhfyrd move back up the mountain to make sure that everything was fine while Rol examined the map to determine their next steps.

According to the map, they would move across the valley and over some small hills to another set of mountains on the other side. It would be best to arrive there by nightfall. Covering that distance was an ambitious goal, but they did not want to be stuck in the valley at night, especially with rain coming, as indicated by the dark clouds heading their way. Walking swiftly and eating while on the move, they saw a clump of tall trees in the distance and decided that was their target. They believed the trees would provide shelter without attracting lightning in the mostly-open valley. It had started to rain, but so far there were no flashes of light in this storm, which meant that they could walk in the open and camp under the trees safely. They walked on through the day.

By the time they reached their supposed oasis, the storm was raging—and it was obvious that Rol, Kearth, and Fhfyrd would be soaked through the entire night unless they found better cover. Instead of settling in, they kept moving and headed toward the base of the cliffs they had seen not long ago in the daylight, prior to the sudden storm. In the dark they thought they could still make out the large shape of the cliffs, but their position was difficult to confirm, as the storm clouds blocked the moon and stars. Their plan was to at least get near the cliffs and hope they would provide protection from the terrible rainstorm—if they were extremely fortunate, they might find a dry cave.

The three of them fumbled past each other, and over and around boulders, until they came to the side of the cliffs. From what they could tell, the rock face rose to the sky, although they couldn't really see how high it soared. At least for the time being, huddled close to the steep rock wall, they were protected somewhat from the rain.

Still, the rain poured down, eventually soaking everything they had, everything they were. Then the rain stopped.

And the bears came.

CHAPTER 17

HOLD ON

As the moon peeked from behind the clouds, it lit up a small hill in the distance behind the three travelers, and they saw the shapes.

Small at first. But as the shapes moved closer, they grew much larger. And they did not look friendly. A quick glance was enough for Rol and his companions to understand that there were fifteen or so moving creatures. They were bears, they were large bears, they were headed purposefully toward the travelers, and there was no protection from them. All three would be trapped between the wild animals and the sheer rock wall. Fhfyrd started moving as quickly as he could along the side of the mountain, looking for any kind of anything the three of them could use to protect themselves. If they found a cave, maybe they would be able to block the entrance. If they could climb the wall, maybe that would be enough to escape claws and teeth.

Fhfyrd, Kearth, and Rol, in that order, kept moving. All they were sure of was that the cliff wall went straight up. They continued passing along the wall, looking for a foothold or handhold so they could attempt to scale the side. But there was nothing other than the sheer, flat, smooth surface, much to their disappointment.

Occasional glances over their shoulders, and the packs on their backs, showed that the beasts were getting closer. The trio mentally steeled themselves, waiting for the attack. Just when they felt the situation to be beyond dire—and hearing the rustle of the bears barreling through wet bushes nearby—two ropes dropped down in front of them along the cliff. Just a few more steps to reach the ropes. Given the circumstances, it did not matter where the ropes came from or who or what had dropped them, only that they were there.

Rol ordered the other two to grab the ropes and start scaling the side of the cliff. Because he had started their journey and directed their travels, he believed it was his responsibility to protect and give them a better chance to survive. Kearth and Fhfyrd argued with him. They did not want to be the ones grabbing the ropes, leaving Rol behind.

A voice from above called down to them, saying, "Stop arguing. Grab the ropes."

Rol said flatly, "Go. Now. Live."

Kearth and Fhfyrd knew that this was their only chance. As they each grabbed a surprisingly dry rope and held on, immediately aware of the weight of their heavy packs, they were pulled up, although slowly.

Kearth and Fhfyrd held on and tried to climb by pulling up the ropes with their arms. They did not know how long the ropes were and how long it would take them to get to safety, or even who was pulling them up. Using their feet and legs, they pushed slightly away from the rocks so that it should have been easier to be hauled up. They saw a third rope drop, and they knew that Rol, too, would be pulled out of harm's way.

As Fhfyrd and Kearth looked down, they saw the bears advancing rapidly on Rol. He managed to grab the rope near him with one hand and was quickly pulled off the ground. The tangle of voices from above—and seemingly not far away—cried out, "Hold on, hold on, hold on to the ropes! Tight as you can!"

Rol held on to his rope with both hands just as a bear came after him with a speed that was jolting. The bear's long claws dug into his pack as Rol continued to grasp the rope that was now wrapped around both of his arms, which meant that he could hold on but not climb. He would have to rely on others to pull him up, assuming he could continue his grip.

With one large bear still hanging on to Rol with its

claws dug deep into his backpack, another attacked with its claws reaching for the back of Rol's right leg. The claws just missed as Rol somehow managed to swing both of his legs upward, away from certain injury and pain.

The second bear was much more aggressive than the first. As the claw swipes came closer and closer to their target, Rol was being yanked up the rope but almost came loose. His arms slipped because of the weight of the bear still hanging on, and then the beast reached out with a powerful back paw to lash at Rol, trying to get a better grasp.

Another attack came from the left. This time it was a bite at Rol's left foot, which missed by a hair's breadth. In the next moment, claws tore into Rol's lower right leg and he felt a large wound open up. He could not yell, he could not think, he could not breathe. He just held on, feeling as though all air had escaped his lungs. He could do nothing but cling to the rope. There was yet another attack—this one with claws prying the waterskin from Rol's side while also grabbing on to the rope and pulling him down.

The unseen angels above shouted and tried to pull Rol up. The massive and terrible beasts below clawed at his plaything body to pull him down. It was a tug-of-war, and Rol was the prize. He had no control, and yet he held on the best he could, his grip slipping slightly as he tried to remember how to breathe.

Rol twisted his body and kicked his legs back and forth any way he could to knock the beast off his pack. He looked down to see the fearsome creatures that would not stop until he was theirs. He heard a faint but familiar voice an infinite rope-length away, directly above him.

"I have to try. If I don't, they will take him," the voice said.

Immediately, he felt a sharp pain to his right ear as the back part folded over toward the front and then snapped back in place.

Rol heard a yelp from a beast below, and he smiled sadly. A painful sensation on his left side came next, this time down his left arm. Rol took a moment to reflect on his situation. It appeared that someone was throwing objects at him from above to put him out of his misery. It was a charitable thought but one that made him struggle even more, fighting to survive.

Rol suddenly felt the rush of many objects flying through the air from above, and he heard the wails of the bears below. He then realized that the objects were rocks—large rocks—thrown down to keep the bears away. Unfortunately, one hit him crushingly on the top of his left shoulder, loosening his grip. He was now holding on with one arm, the other hanging limply at his side.

Large rocks rained down incessantly. Surely, they were meant for the bears, not him, Rol thought. Surely, Fhfyrd would notice Rol still hanging on and wanting to live. With one last, desperate act of fighting for his life, Rol reached out with his left hand to grab the rope. His scream of pain shattered the night through the cacophony of sounds above, below, and around him, but he held on as tight as his survival instincts could muster.

More animal yelps followed, and then a release as the bear latched on to his pack won . . . and lost. Rol's pack ripping from his shoulders meant that the bear's weight was too much. The bear landed flat on its back and remained there, unmoving.

Seeing multiple bears lying motionless beneath him, Rol closed his eyes in hopes of remembering the scene always. He was quickly pulled higher and higher. In his fog of pain, he realized that he might just make it through the night, although the night was rapidly fading away. Just before reaching safety, Rol blacked out. In his unconsciousness, his grip on the rope loosened. He fell through the night.

CHAPTER 18

A PROPER BURIAL

A day later, in a solemn ceremony, Kearth and Fhfyrd buried him.

Him being the bear that had held on to Rol's pack for so long. The animal that in the end had served as a softer-than-the-ground landing spot when Rol lost his grip on the rope and tumbled down the side of the cliff. It was the bear that had unknowingly saved Rol's life, and that Rol's companions determined should have a proper burial even though it had tried to finish off their friend.

Later that day, Rol awoke from his pain-filled slumber and was able to stay awake long enough for Kearth to recount how Fhfyrd shot two arrows to take down the largest of the beasts, unfortunately also skimming one of Rol's ears and arms.

"Quite sorry 'bout that," interjected Fhfyrd, lovingly patting his bow.

It was the large rocks thrown from the top of the cliff that inflicted most of the damage on the attackers, once the rescuers above realized that in addition to pulling Rol up, they should also somehow remove the bears from the situation. Otherwise, the rope, or Rol's arms, would break from the immense weight.

"But who . . . ?" managed Rol, and then his eyes rested upon the wild red-brown hair and beard of the leader of the warrior tribe known as the Eye Lenders. A smile from Rol, a nod to his familiar rescuer, then grayness just before he heard Fhfyrd say, "Of course. Now I get it. You're Highlanders. By the way, it's pronounced *Feared*."

And then everything went blank.

A Proper Burial

"Where?" questioned Rol weakly.

"You're in a makeshift tent," answered Kearth, "someplace in some mountains somewhere to be exact, as far as I can tell. You've been unconscious for two pages . . . er . . . *days*."

It took a few more days for Rol to heal enough to travel. The warriors had said their "bye-goods" two days prior, leaving Rol, Kearth, and Fhfyrd alone in the camp.

After Rol had been recovering for almost a week, Kearth was excited for him to finally be mostly conscious. He was eager to consult his fellow traveler about an important and long-winded map question that had been building for some time.

"Why are we following this map," Kearth asked. "because it seems to take us from one questionable area to the next, and I realize that we're following it appropriately according to the landmarks the best we can, but it's not a very straight line, if you know what I mean, and it looks as though we're wandering back and forth over and around mountain-hills and over and through and around lakes and rivers, taking a roundabout way to where we need to go, and also, too, plus, in addition, what about this route at the bottom, and why didn't you take it from the beginning, and now why don't we find a way to it, because wouldn't it mean a straight path, or at least straighter path, to the journey's end?"

Rol followed along with the question the best he could and then let Kearth catch his breath before replying.

"I'll answer the best way I know how," said Rol, propping himself up on one arm. "First, if I hadn't gone the more roundabout route, I would not have met you or Fhfyrd. I may have been home by now. Don't imagine for a moment that I don't wonder about that every day. Second, I don't know exactly why this map route is so important. Maybe it was exactly so that I could meet you two, or maybe it was meant for me to be fully life-challenged after all the teachings from my uncle. I just know that this was the map that DaTerrin left me and that we must follow it to the end, even when it changes course from what appears to be a straight line."

"Well," said Kearth, "I suggest that maybe, possibly, probably, we should not follow this map. And maybe, possibly, and definitely probably, we should just head toward our final destination directly, assuming that is your home."

Fhfyrd countered, "Wait. I think that we should listen to Rol. He's the one who started this trek, and he's the one who knows most about it. He's the reason we're on this journey, and he, as far as I'm concerned, knows where we're going."

"In my opinion," rebutted Kearth, "I feel that we end up spending days in different areas, and that is not the best use of our time. My time, frankly. Although it has been quite an adventure—and I sincerely mean that—I, for one, am anxious to find out where it ends up."

Rol answered, "You have to trust me on this. I know that we are going in the right direction. And I have this incredible feeling that this is what we are meant to do. At least this is what *I* am meant to do. I can't speak for either of you. I just know this is my journey, and it's important for me to follow the path that we are on right now—this 'Pancreas' leading me forward. This is the right thing to do."

"Well, certainly we can cut out one or two of these places," said Kearth, pointing to the frayed map and apparently missing the "Pancreas" mention. "It looks like we still have a long way to go, and there are many areas to cover. We've already been through so much, haven't we? Haven't we been on this adventure together for a long time? I know that you started out on your own, Rol, but it has been a long time that we've been with you. I'm getting tired. I'm looking for the end. It's funny that I don't even know what that will bring us, what that offers us, at the end, but I'm ready for it."

Rol said, "I'm not forcing you to stay, although I wish you would. You're right that we have gone to many different areas, and maybe it would be nice to travel directly and get there quicker, to the end. But I don't know if that's the right thing to do. In fact, it feels as though it is *not* the right thing to do, and I've really had to go with my feelings all along the way. I've had to go by my inner feelings, and it's worked fairly well so far, even though we've had some struggles. We survived, and here we are. Has it been easy? Has it been comfortable? Has it been pleasurable every moment of every day? I can't say that it has.

"But I do know that I don't know what else I would be doing at this time. I'm hoping that the map will lead to my family soon. So if I'm wandering—I am wandering with a purpose. Even if we are moving back and forth from one place to another, then at least the general direction is forward. That's all I can do for now. I can't ask you to travel with me because I don't know your destiny, and I'm not even sure of my own destiny. It's up to you. It's up to you both. You can choose to continue for a little while and change your mind later. You can choose to leave now. It's completely up to you, and I accept your decision."

Kearth paused and then responded, "I'll think about it. I will think very hard about it. It's getting dark, and I am very tired. I'm tired of talking, I guess. Tired of thinking. We can discuss this tomorrow."

With that, Kearth went off to one side of the small clearing and arranged his belongings for the night, lay down, and quickly fell asleep. Fhfyrd and Rol stayed up a little longer, settling next to a small fire that was not quite warm enough. Not large enough and not bright enough, either, though it was nonetheless a nice enough spot in which to just sit and think and talk awhile more.

“What do you want to do?” Rol asked Fhfyrd.

Fhfyrd didn’t answer immediately. There were a few moments of utter quietness. He then said, “I will continue with you, and with Kearth, if possible. I agree that this seems to be the right thing to do. I don’t know what he’s going through or what he’s expecting. I thought we were all of the same mind in this, but if he’s tired of this journey and he wants to settle down, then that’s what he needs to do. I think it best to let him bring up the subject again. We’ll see how he is in the morning and if he wants to travel on or would prefer to stay longer in this area. It’s something that he needs to come to terms with himself. He must make his own decision. We’ll just keep our traveling plans and see what he decides to do.”

Rol agreed, saying, “You’re right. We’ll just have to wait and see.” The two of them sat silently, gazing at the small fire, not saying anything, not expecting the other to say anything. Just sitting and thinking. Thinking over the past few months and what they had left behind. Wondering what they would face the next day and the day after and the day after. It was a thoughtful silence, a good silence, a much-needed silence. Until Kearth broke the silence with his snoring.

"I guess he's not thinking about it too hard at the moment," Rol said, and they both laughed quietly. The fire died down and Fhfyrd nodded off in a sitting position. Rol tried not to think any more about what had been said that day, at least for the time being. Soon enough, his eyelids closed as well.

CHAPTER 19

VOICES AND HORSES

The following morning, after breakfast, Kearth packed his belongings.

He said to Rol and Fhfyrd, "What are you waiting for? Let's go."

Later that day, Rol and all the travelers who had decided to continue traveling with him—which was both of them—walked through the tiny hamlet of Grubbyfingerston. It was a pleasant place, other than the many overweight rats in residence. And the carnivorous butterflies.

As Rol and his small party of two, obviously not counting himself, passed through the hamlet, looking very much like they were just passing through, they were stopped by a group of several townsfolk. The locals told them that as obvious passers-through, they should realize that the way to the North would be the safest route out of town, as long as they stayed on the Path of General Goodness. Straying from the path would mean absolute death, or at least the possibility thereof. Or *thereto*. The townsfolk could never remember which, grammar-wise. In any case, they said, "Do not take the side road to the East." They explained that in addition to making the travelers' shoes and boots unbelievably muddy, it will lead to the Terrible Ruins of Ultimate Despair, which most of them believed was the correct name of the place, although they could not all agree on that. Even venturing down the eastern road could mean certain . . . something. They could never remember exactly what. They just never went that way. They knew it had to do with the dead speaking, but that was about it. Foggy memories but dire warnings. "The dead speaking." Wasn't that bad enough? Who wanted that, especially after a dire warning?

"Not me," the townsfolk said collectively. And they said it loudly. And often. And direly.

"Of course, nobody ever returns from the Horrible Ruins of Great Despair. Or is it Definite Despair? Or . . ." They could never remember the actual name, they said.

For the record, it is important to note that only on rare occasions did the townsfolk speak all the words at the same time. Generally, various individuals spoke the same words at different times, with the sum effect of their speaking with a single voice.

Of course, Rol was fantastically curious, and he and his brave companions took the road to the East, to the ruins. To the warned-against, dead-speaking, ruined ruins. Truth be told, they never returned to Grubbyfingerston. Ever. The townsfolk were right . . . again. All part of an amazing, practically self-fulfilling series of legends linked to the ruins. All part of squishy statistics that nobody ever confirmed by asking whether people actually never left the ruins or simply never returned to Grubbyfingerston to file a report upon returning from said ruins. Who would want to visit a town like Grubbyfingerston a second time anyway, what with all the dire warnings and nonsense?

As Rol, Fhfyrd, and Kearth walked down the perilous, treacherous, and surprisingly beautifully scenic path they realized that the ruins were a far distance in the distance. In fact, at least three days' travel farther. At least that's what the signs indicated.

Specifically, the first one said: "Three days of heart-breaking slogging through a painfully muddy and unkempt road. Why do it? Turn around now and stay in town while you think it over."—Sponsored by Jasper's Free-Flowing Tavern and Overwhelmingly Comfortable Inn.

Another chimed in: "Ruins—you know the ones—only three days away. Three tortuous days in unbearably arduous conditions. Why not have a bite and a cool drink before you go?"—Smitty's Good Eats Parlour and Part-Time Day Spa.

And there was one more: "Three days to certain death . . . if you make it that long."—Skinny, the ruins hermit.

Not concerned about "certain death," Rol and his faithful companions trudged on. For two and a half days, they trudged on. They trudged, trudged, and trudged some more. They tried to tread lightly, but it turned quickly back to trudging. After two and a half days—during which they stopped a few times to eat, rest, snack, pull their boots from the mud, rest, snack, trudge, look through their packs wondering where all the snacks went, pull their packs from the mud, rest, and take in the eye-and-mind-pleasing scenery—they caught sight of the ruins. They realized that they were indeed beholding the Great Ruins of Definite Despair—and the townsfolk had been mostly correct, because a sign at the side of the road said: "Great Ruins of Definite Despair straight ahead, one-half mile. Congratulations on not being dead yet."

And still they trudged on. Within moments, a man accosted them. A skinny man. A skinny man they assumed was Skinny, the ruins hermit. And they said so. And Skinny the hermit he was, in fact, and he said so to confirm it. And the four of them made small talk, and smiled a lot, and shook hands, and patted each other on the back like old friends. And they were old friends, just not each other's. As that realization settled upon them, there was an awkward silence, except for the even more awkward sound of Skinny's old bones creaking. Then Skinny broke the silence saying, "Did I ever mention that I hear the dead speak?"

Rol wondered what he meant by "ever mention," as they had only met moments before, but he went along with Skinny, saying, "But didn't we just meet . . . er . . . no, you didn't mention it, Skinny."

"Well, in that case, let me tell you about it, over here, by these (suspenseful buildup of silence, crescendoing into a wave of even greater silence) . . . RUINS!"

He led them, trudgingly, to the ruins. Rol could make out that they had once been some kind of building or rocky structure—possibly a castle, although castles were rare those days and had been even more rare in times past. The collapsed building was not huge compared to other ancient structures, but the boulders used to construct it were large and heavy. It looked like it had collapsed, possibly because of a groundshake, some other disaster, or even an attack long ago. In fact, it must have originally been constructed a very long time ago due to the terras grass growing on the tops and sides of the boulders, which terras grass is not likely to do without being threatened by force. Force for terras grass being harsh words, as they are a very sensitive species, if you can call grass a species, which you can't.

Rol, Kearth, Fhfyrd, and Skinny moved even closer to take in the sight before them. Skinny pointed to the collapsed structure. "That's where I hear the voices," he explained. "Although I don't hear them at the moment."

"What do they sound like?" asked Fhfyrd, suddenly feeling a chill on the back of his neck, attributing it to the hauntedness of the ruins and not realizing it was Kearth blowing air while pretending he wasn't.

"They sound exactly like voices," replied Skinny.

"Oh, well, that clears things up," Fhfyrd replied, annoyed. Annoyed because he was expecting a more profound answer—and because he had caught on to Kearth's antics.

Standing in the shadow of the ruins, they waited and listened for the voices. Skinny sat down on a large rock, beckoning the others to come closer. They listened. Rol sat down on ruins rubble nearby, and Kearth and Fhfyrd did the same. They listened again. Skinny stood up and brushed off the large rock where he had been sitting, then lay down with his back on the rock. More listening. Kearth cracked his thumb knuckles, which made everyone's ears perk up temporarily. They waited and listened. Skinny fell asleep and snored loudly, overpowering any ruins voices that might have been heard at that time.

Rol spoke up, over the snoring. "I think we should be

going," he said.

At that, Skinny sat straight up and said, "Did you hear that?"

"Hear what?" said Rol. "I didn't hear anything."

"I heard it plain as day," replied Skinny. "It was a voice. It said, 'We should be going,' or something like that. That's what I hear whenever I bring someone out here. I wonder what it means. It must be a sign that the dead want to leave this place. I must tell the others that I heard it again." Off he ran, as fast as his old bones would allow.

Less than a week later, as Rol and his two traveling companions were still talking about Skinny and walking through a nice clearing in a tangled forest, they came upon three horses, which coincidently—or so it seemed— was their number, too. The healthy-appearing horses were tied up to two tall oakish trees, with plentiful green-as-could-be grass growing nearby—apparently for food. With lengthy ropes tied loosely around their necks so they could move almost freely, the horses had plenty of roaming room. They also had a number of large wooden buckets of water to drink. It was almost too good to be true.

"Almost," thought Fhfyrd aloud, in the direction of the horses.

Curiously, there was also a handmade wooden sign—

actually, three signs—on the two trees where the horses were tied. Each said: "Free horses. Take one. But just one each."

Rol, Kearth, and Fhfyrd looked at each other in the same astounded fashion. It was one of those looks that went something like: "Free horses, take one? Free horses? Who would do such a thing, and why are there free horses out in the tangled forest that we have been walking through for days? And, of course, it just so happens that there are three, which is exactly the number that we need. What? Who? How? Why? What again?"

Being good fellow citizens in a forest that was not their home territory, the traveling companions decided that they should discuss that it seemed a little too easy to get free horses. Each had a question, and those questions from Rol, Fhfyrd, and Kearth—in that order—were: "Who would be giving us free horses?" "Why is someone giving horses away, and is their real motive to stage some kind of attack when we are distracted?" "Shouldn't we just go ahead and take them—the sign said 'Free,' didn't it—and isn't it time for lunch?"

Having investigated the general vicinity and not seeing anyone, they decided the free horses they undoubtedly were meant to have should be taken. So they took them. Conveniently, each horse had a saddle as well as bags. Inconveniently, the bags were empty rather than full of coins or food, though they were handy in terms of stashing their traveling belongings, nice and tidy like.

The journeyers thumb wrestled to see who would get to choose his horse first. Each chose a particular horse for a particular reason, although Kearth ended up with last choice, meaning he didn't have a choice at all.

With first-pick rights, Rol took the tallest one, a black stallion with a white mark on its hindquarters in the shape of some . . . something. He couldn't quite make it out, although if he closed one eye and looked upside-down with the other, the shape could possibly have been something recognizable, though he wasn't sure exactly what. Instinctively yet oddly, he felt close to that specific horse after walking up to it slowly and making friends with it to the extent you can make friends with a horse. Some people (you know, those kinds of people) might argue that you can make great friends with horses once you get to know them, and they get to know you. There are others (you know how they are) who might say that horses are really just there to carry items and pull things, as well as transport you—and what kind of person wants a horse as a friend anyway?

Rol felt the correct thing to do was to make friends with his chosen horse. So he did what he felt most natural in that particular situation. Grabbing a handful of grass near his feet, he offered it to the beautiful beast, which ate it noncommittally. Rol and the horse were then friends. He was friends with a horse that was as black as night but with a white shape he couldn't quite identify. It would come to him at some point, though. Rol called his new traveling companion MoonBlack. At the mention of the name, MoonBlack rose up on his hind legs and whinnied loudly, his forelegs pawing at the air in a show of strength, balance, and readiness for action.

It was classic.

Fhfyrd chose the second tallest though most massive horse. It was quite active on his end of the rope, solid muscle through and through. He was a rich chestnut-brown color and had greenish-blue eyes, a striking combination. Truthfully, had he been first, Fhfyrd would have chosen the black horse, though he would have named it something else, but that was the way things went when you were not great at thumb wrestling. He had never thought about making friends with a horse until that day, but it seemed the right approach—and one that could come in handy later. Fhfyrd offered a handful of grass to his new mode of transportation, which accepted it graciously. The name Crush seemed fitting and Fhfyrd said it out loud, though this time there was no reaction such as the one seen moments earlier.

The third horse was white. Just white. And some speckles of gray. But mostly white. Enough white to be called

Snowflake or Snowy or Snowfall or some other name describing the bright-white nature of the beast. Going against the grain, Kearth called the horse GrayFlake, but when he saw Rol's and Fhfyrd's expressions, he quickly changed the name to WhiteHide, which was weeks later changed to WinterSnow because of a trademark dispute, although nobody was ever able to determine what all the fuss was about.

The next few moments were an excited flurry of activity as each journeying adventurer transferred his traveling items from his pack, around his waist, or tied to his elbows, to the nice, new pack on his new free horse. There had not been such excitement in the air for a few days. It was as though the trio had been given gifts—*gift horses* to be exact—just when they would come in most handy.

Still somewhat dubious about the whole free horse thing, Rol decided just before they left the area that he should take at least one of the "Free horses. Take one. But just one each." signs for good measure. He put the sign in his bag in case he had to prove that the three of them were the beneficiaries of some nice forest dweller who was giving away free horses.

"You never know," he said.

Then Rol, Fhfyrd, and Kearth climbed onto their horses. Rol and Kearth climbed up rather clumsily. Neither had been on a horse since his early younger days, and the so-called horses at that time were really small ponies. But both made it up nonetheless. The three of them decided to ride swiftly down the wide path to the next town, for no other reason than to ride swiftly because they could.

Fhfyrd pointed his previously valuable-as-a-walking-stick walking stick forward and yelled, "Honor and glory!" He then launched his horse forward with the speed of a horse being launched forward by someone who wanted to make a great launching for the benefit of himself, as well as his soon-to-be riding companions on their way to another phase in their great adventure.

Kearth, second in line, let Fhfyrd travel approximately five hoof steps. Then, loud enough to be heard through the just-beginning-though-thunderous-nonetheless hoof steps, he shouted, "Wait!"

CHAPTER 20

A GIANT PREDICAMENT

Fhfyrd's horse halted immediately, throwing his rider up and over its head and onto the hard ground ahead.

Rol, interested in this interesting development, stayed out of the way to see what was going to happen next. By the time Fhfyrd was able to get back onto his horse and turn around, Rol was even more intrigued. He had to hold himself back from saying a word, lest he change the outcome of the situation in any way. It was too much to bear, but he had to let things play out.

Mounted superiorly on Crush, Fhfyrd trotted back and said, not unhappily but not happily, either, "What? What is it? Why did you tell me to wait?"

"I was curious," explained Kearth. "'Honor and glory!' Where did that come from? Not that I am complaining in any way, but it was something unexpected, and I didn't want to lose the opportunity to ask you where that came from. I mean, I have never, until that very moment, heard you utter such a cry—and I quickly realized that if I did not ask the question immediately, I risked losing the moment and would never know. So what is it? Why 'Honor and glory!'?"

Obviously frustrated, Fhfyrd replied, "Why? That's it? You stopped me to ask 'Why?'" Red-faced now—not from the swift riding, or even the turning around and riding back, but from exasperation—Fhfyrd did all he could to resist throwing his walking stick turned mighty pointer at his riding companion.

"Why did I say what I said?" questioned Fhfyrd, drawing in a long breath, which made Rol nervous because he feared Fhfyrd was choking. "Simple. Have you ever wanted to say something but were never afforded the chance until one exciting moment when the words just came out of your mouth without warning, and you finally fulfilled one of your greatest wishes? Have you ever had a moment like that? Well, I just did. It was exciting and grand and over before I knew it, but it happened and then someone—you—had to say 'Wait!' And then it all came to a halt. A *halt*, I say, because that's exactly what my horse did, and I have the cracked ribs to prove it. Then I had to turn this mighty beast around, which is not as easy as one might expect, and return to discuss the issue with you, which is not an issue that should be discussed anyway. It should have just happened, and I should have had my moment, and now that I'm here, I wonder—does that satisfy your curiosity?"

"It does. Oh, it does," said Kearth. "I just wanted to know because the phrase 'Honor and glory!' was such an appropriate declaration at the time, and forgive me for halting a key moment in your storied life, but I just had to know before I forgot and lost the moment forever, as I mentioned. So let us carry on, and carry the phrase 'Honor and glory!' in our hearts and the back of our throats forever! Honor and glory!" yelled Kearth, and he sped off down the path, in the lead, just the way he wanted.

"You're mocking me!" yelled Fhfyrd, and sped off after Kearth, catching and passing him, dust temporarily turning Kearth's horse into BrownHide, which was not in conflict with any trademarks and would have been safe to use.

Rol shook his head, smiled, and followed the dusty cloud of a trail. He was thinking *"Honor and glory!"* but not saying it aloud, as he was busy holding on to MoonBlack's rope and hoping that falling off a horse was not in his immediate future.

As they rode along, the travelers failed to notice the three bandits at the side of the path, off in the forest a few paces. The bad guys had been waiting all day for someone to take the bait of their trap but were currently sleeping soundly, missing all the commotion. They soon woke up and found themselves horseless, prompting one of the bandits to say, "Oh no. Not again."

The travelers urged their horses straight down the wide path, thinking that traveling on horseback was much easier than walking.

"Much, much easier," Kearth would have said had he been asked, though he wasn't.

In fact, traveling on horseback was so much easier that all three of them had almost forgotten how challenging and tiring it was to travel on foot, not that they were retro-complaining. They rode all through that day and into the night. Rol, Fhfyrd, and Kearth were so overjoyed, they could have kept going like that for miles. But they knew the horses needed something to eat and drink. As they rode along looking for a place where they could semi-safely and semi-comfortably spend the night, they realized they didn't have food for the horses and the ground nearby was more brambly than grassy, much to the chagrin of their kind beasts.

Soon enough, though, they found an incredible place to spend the evening. Incredible because even though the night was black, with just a hint of moon, they could see that crescent reflecting on a beautiful pond ahead of them.

They decided to spend the night next to the ripple-free water, close to the horses, which were tied to bushes with a large patch of grass nearby to munch.

It was such a blissful night, they did not keep watch, feeling completely at peace where they were. Truthfully, they were all too tired from the ride for any of them to stand guard. Unfortunately, that had the potential to be a big mistake.

It wasn't long before the three travelers were at last asleep, and possibly their three horses, too—although it was hard to tell since horses can sleep standing up—and because they don't often mention any unusual dreams they might have such as holding a great treasure in their hooves and then waking to find it was all a dream even though it felt as though "it was right there, I could feel it."

Two small giants came to the small pond to fetch water. The reason for fetching water that late at night, although not important, was probably diabolical, knowing giants, without unfairly stereotyping in the least.

Having excellent night vision, the giants immediately saw the horses but did not notice the three travelers, who were hidden by the foliage. One of the horses had woken up and was looking at his front left hoof with a "But it was right there, I could feel it" look of dismay on his face, which was lost on the giants who were not in the mood to debate the sleeping or dreaming habits of horses.

Contrary to popular belief, almost all giants have a terrible sense of smell. They instead rely on their strong vision, which is surprising, because most stories portray giants as having a strong sense of smell but terrible vision, unquestionably because giants own and display rather large noses. But those stories are likely about mountain giants, and in this case the journeyers were about to meet *hill* giants—who, upon arriving at the pond and seeing the unfamiliar creatures, had a decision to make.

The decision that giants generally make in all situations is to blindly attack without cause or much thought. So attack the hill giants did.

For these particular giants, the meaning of *attack* was slightly different to them from what it might have meant to other creatures, because as younger giants, they had little experience in attacking. No experience at all would be a more accurate description, as these particular giant youngers had experienced battle only by way of minimal training. And that was fortunate for Rol, his friends, and especially their horses.

Although the giants were slightly larger in size, but not when it came to think-ability, than the horses they approached, because of their minimal training they were not particularly dangerous other than the possibility of bumping into one of the horses and knocking it down. The giants were almost comical in the way they shuffled, and they were as slow in moving as they were in thinking.

One of the giants approached Kearth's horse and started wrestling it. Grabbing the horse around the neck with both arms, the giant tried to swing his weight around in order to pull the horse down, thereby winning the contest, which was important to giants, especially younger ones. Horses are not familiar with wrestling, though, and apparently don't like the activity. Giants don't come in contact with horses often, and other creatures, other than other giants, are not large enough for them to wrestle with. It was a strange occurrence, with a giant wrestling a horse and neither knowing what to do, other than the horse knowing to kick, which was not part of the giant's wrestling training at all.

It didn't take long for Rol and his companions to wake up, because of the sounds of a horse versus a hill giant, and the other giant cheering on his friend. Kearth almost immediately came to his senses, because it was his horse that was being wrestled, yet it was such an odd sight that he didn't know what to do, other than stare and tilt his head slightly. None of the journeyers expected to be woken up by a giant conflict, so it was a tense yet sleepy moment, with the journeying onlookers rubbing their eyes, trying to determine the best game plan.

Fhfyrd decided to spring into action. Waving his sword, which had not been used at all this adventure other than to cut ropes or help him look intimidating, he yelled loudly and chased after the small giants. Kearth followed, flailing his arms about. Rol grabbed his Battlestick and joined the fray. The giants, intent on the horse wrestling, saw the unexpected creatures scrambling fiercely toward them and ran off, wide-eyed—one heading in one direction, and the other, the opposite way. It was almost laughable, if they had not been such potentially dangerous opponents. The three travelers—now courageous giant-chasers—rested and watched for any sign of the giants returning. Then, as the sun began to rise and create blinding reflections on the lake, they gathered their belongings and decided to leave the area quickly, just in case.

CHAPTER 21

"DO YOU HAPPEN TO HAVE ANY . . ."

After a good ride that day, the trio decided to walk alongside their horses awhile to give them a break.

"I had a horse like this once," said Kearth, out of nowhere.

"You had a horse?" replied Fhfyrd.

"Yes, it was a one-of-a-kind horse. Dark black, just like that one of Rol's. He was magnificent. I actually have nice memories of when I used to have that horse, although I never learned to ride him."

"What do you mean used to have? You don't have him at home? Why not?"

"Well, it didn't work out. It just didn't exactly work out between us."

"What do you mean it didn't work out between you?"

"I . . . I didn't know what to feed him, OK?"

"What do you mean you didn't know what to feed him?"

"I had a horse and I didn't know what to feed him. Now I don't have him any longer. He uh . . ."

"No, wait. Don't tell me. You didn't know what to feed him . . . and he . . . died?"

"No, not at all. He ran away. Of course he didn't, you know . . . of course not. Not my horse. No, he ran away."

"So then he ran away because you didn't feed him. I see."

"Well, no. He didn't run away because I didn't feed him. He actually ran away because of what I was trying to feed him."

"What were you trying to feed him?"

"Well . . . it's . . . difficult to explain."

"So it was a good thing that he ran away, then?"

"Yes, I believe it was."

"I think that's enough. Thanks for the story. Next time, why don't you keep your horse stories to yourself?"

"I can try again with these horses."

"No, you can't."

"I just need a few ingredients. Do you happen to have any . . ."

And before he could finish, MoonBlack took off, causing Rol to chase after him as fast as he could, proving that although horses don't necessarily understand everything that people say, they can usually tell what they mean.

Late that afternoon, the three companions sat in a circle around the warming fire, with their horses on the fringe of the camp Fhfyrd had set up. Even though they rode a long way on horseback, they still were tentative about meeting up with giants in this region. Their plan was to find a place to rest during the day and ride at night. It was safe to have a fire, as it likely would not be seen while it was still light.

"Tell us about your parents, Kearth," said Rol, curious about his background.

"I don't remember my mother," replied Kearth after a pause. "She died when I was very young, from what I was told. They say her hair was golden, like the late afternoon sun, and she smelled of roses. I wish I knew her . . ." he trailed off. "Then there was my father. He was a great adventurer. He never left the house except to do chores, but, oh, the adventures he had! He was always having adventures." Kearth grew quiet, remembering.

"Wait. I thought you said that you remembered your mother saying that she didn't want you to hang around thieves and . . . you know."

"Who said that?" said a perplexed Kearth.

"Who said what?" said a very perplexed Rol.

"Who said that comment about hanging around

thieves?" said a frustrated Kearth.

"I did, of course," said a very frustrated Rol. "I'm right here. You saw me say it."

"It's just that I don't see your name next to it," said an accusing Kearth.

"My name next to what?" said an accused Rol.

"You know, when someone says something, and their name is next to what they said. I don't see it for that one," said an exasperated Kearth, still trying to explain.

"I don't under—" started Rol, but he was interrupted by the sound of a storm approaching. "We'll get back to this," he whispered. But they never really did.

It was night. It was dark. It was foggy. It was raining. It was a rain-fog to end all rain-fogs, and they were riding through it on horses that were not happy to be there. Wet horses that conveniently paired up well with the journeyers' wet belongings, few though they were. Wet clothes they were wearing, wet clothes they had packed. Wet rope, wet food, wet map, wet torches, wet everything and all. It was a new phase in an otherwise grandiose adventure. A good, cleansing phase.

If you liked mushy, gushy, gloomy misery. Not misery in everything, all together and forever. Just misery in this particular moment . . . and the few before. And, unfortunately, what looked like it would be the same situation for the next few. The otherwise in-decent-spirits trio happened to be headed right into the middle of the storm, having just passed through the outskirts. It wasn't "poor, poor little ol' wretched me" misery, but it was close.

On second thought, it was exactly "poor, poor little ol' wretched me" misery—but nobody would say that out loud, although grunting hints to that effect were running rampant. Even Rol, who theretofore had been positive about the outcome of every situation, was wondering about any bright sides to this one. Any silver linings. Any rainbows. Anything that he and his companions could hold on to for the next few moments, days—whatever it took to get out of there and to a better place.

"Remember that time when it wasn't dark and gloomy?" questioned Rol semi-cheerfully, with just a hint of strained optimism in his tired and worn voice. "When we rode our mighty steeds as though there was no tomorrow? And we traveled to places unknown and met people unknown and encountered a few bizarre animals that were previously unknown, at least to us?" Pause. No answer. Continue. "And we laughed and rode and laughed even more? Remember that time?"

"No," came the downtrodden response, followed by something sailing through the air to rest thuddingly on the side of Rol's soggy cheek. He imagined a balled-up hunk of stale bread, but he couldn't be sure and was too tired to verbally investigate.

"And we knew that we must be going in the right direction, following the previously dry map, and that we would make it to the end, wherever that end might be?" continued Rol, undaunted. "Remember that us? Not this us but *that* us?"

It might have been a boot nearly missing him, but Rol could only wonder silently about it: *Who had the energy to throw a boot in his direction, and who was so desperate to throw something, that he would sacrifice that which would come in handy later?*

"Anyone see my boot?" came the answer soon enough. "My boot," repeated Kearth, obviously now desperate to find his footwear. "A left one. Brown. Thoroughly soaked all the way through, not that I'm complaining. Anyone?"

"We should stop here," answered Fhfyrd, without actually answering anything, pulling back on the reins slightly to slow his almost-too-tired-to-take-another-step horse. "As good a place as any to rest for the next few hours. Kearth can gather his belongings."

Kearth felt the force of the comment as it headed in his direction, even though he could not see more than an arm's length away.

"B—" was all that came out as the beginning of a standard Kearth rebuttal before he realized it was best not to say a word since he suddenly did feel somewhat embarrassed about the boot thing. And he might need help finding his boot in this soggy, muddy mess, where he found himself, semi-bootless, having just dismounted from his horse.

"We shall rest. So it has been commanded," said Kearth, trying to sarcastically deflect any other comments heading his way.

Rest they did not. Not in the rain-fog that suddenly turned into a downpour, putting a heavier damper on a lousier situation. They could not move because they could not see and they did not want to lose their way or their horses. The living modes of transportation cooperated nicely by just standing still and not stepping on toes or complaining much.

It was a night of nights—memorable, but not in a good way.

"To pass the time we can play a game," said Kearth in the darkness. Rol smiled tiredly, knowingly.

"Sounds just slightly more enjoyable than sitting here in the cold rain and darkness," responded Fhfyrd. "What kind of game?"

"It's a game that doesn't take any talent at all," answered Kearth.

"Well, then, of course—I'm up for that. But first, I was

wondering if you saw the sky before we had this mess of a rainstorm."

"What difference would that make? It was not raining, and then it was. So what?"

"Well, if the sky was reddish-orangish earlier, then maybe it will stop raining soon and be clear in the morning."

"I'm sorry that I didn't make a note of what color the sky was prior to the fog and then pouring rain and now the complete darkness. I know you are supposedly a first-rate tracker, but I don't believe that you could possibly tell, based on the color of the sky, what kind of weather is upcoming. It was red; it was blue; it was green; it had stripes. What difference does it make? How could you know? You must be some kind of sky expert. Does dressing all in black somehow help you tell what kind of weather we're going to have? If you are such an expert, why didn't you take note of the sky conditions yourself, Mr. Sky Guy, so that we could marvel at your weather-predicting skills, instead of asking us, who could not care any less about the color of the sky?"

There was a moment of silence, other than the sound of the rain, which had increased in volume and intensity. Not expecting that kind of reaction in the least from Kearth, Fhfyrd said, "I didn't expect that kind of reaction in the least. Never mind, then. It's a stupid game anyway."

"What game is that?" questioned Kearth.

CHAPTER 22

SMELLS GOOD ENOUGH TO EAT

The fog and rain cleared the next day, and they were able to move on, although it took three full days for their clothes and gear to dry, even after setting all of it near a fire to take advantage of the heat. The mud stayed with them, in wet form and then in dry, throughout the rest of their journey.

With the rain behind them and clear skies ahead, the three travelers were enjoying riding their horses, galloping freely in the wind and trying to make up for lost time.

They smelled the town ahead before they actually saw it.

Moving along happily on horses that desperately needed a bath, each individual rider was not quite as interesting-smelling as the horses he traveled on. Not in the way that horses can often smell, which might not be altogether unpleasant if you like that sort of thing, and some do. But in this case each horse-rider unit was pungent, and yet the smell of the upcoming though unseen town was odoriferously noticeable, if not already tear inducing.

Then they saw it, and the tears undeniably flowed freely.

It was a mess. A nostril-shrieking, eye-blurring, close-your-mouth-or-you-will-regret-it-believe-me kind of mess that forced visitors to not visit and locals not to, either.

It grew worse as the travelers approached. Growing worse was an unfortunate and yet terribly accurate description. The town was a mass of mess that continued to—gulp—feed on itself. Not literally, but it didn't matter because when your mind is reeling and you can't, or rather shouldn't, at all costs, breathe, you lose your sense of everything other than smell, which you suddenly regret ever having, even going all the way back to when you were just born and the sweet smell of Mom hit you like a ton of fragrant roses. If you—as a visitor not staying long, or even short—kept your feet and didn't immediately fall over onto the smell-encrusted ground, you would most likely find your rubbery legs leaving on their own accord and taking you with them, hopefully.

Rol, Kearth, and Fhfyrd did not flee. They calmly leapt frantically down from their horses. Then they quickly, though haphazardly scattered to avoid having their horses fall on them as they collapsed into an unconscious heap. The horses surprised them, though, by gathering the strength left in their rubbery horse legs and leaving on their own horse accord—astonishingly also leaving the packs behind, chaotically scattered on the ground.

So there and then the companions found themselves. Horseless. In Smelton, if you could believe the hand-drawn sign just outside the rubbish-pile-that-may-somehow-be-mistaken-for-a-town. The sign, with its arrow wisely pointing in a direction that was not toward the town stench. The stench, which was actually everywhere, therefore rendering the arrows useless other than to serve as a warning to birds of prey with naturally keen eyesight and the bonus sensibility to understand that an arrow pointing away from a town meant that even always-hungry and not-particular-about-what-they-eat vultures should not want to get involved.

With nothing left to do—already soaked in the putrid air of the place and of little actual sane mind remaining—the three walked into town.

If the outside of the town was disgustingness supreme, the actual inside of the town was remarkably magnificent. The reaction of the travelers went from "Whoa" to "Wow" as the previous unpleasant reeling from the hideous smell became an almost pleasant reeling from the marvelous sight.

Walking toward what was presumably the center of town, with its three-story-high fountain, the three dirty and well-traveled travelers were met with grinning mouths and questioning eyes from everyone they encountered.

Everyone, that is, but a fairly rotund woman in shockingly clean and fashionable clothes, whose expression was pure smile all around. The welcoming committee of one. The mayor of Smelton.

Within a matter of moments, she both apologized for the condition of the outside of the town and explained that the fringes were cleverly covered in trash to keep would-be invaders out while the inner core was beautifully preserved.

"Of course, 'You can't judge a town by its disgusting and appallingly vomit-inducing dung pile of disrespect to almost every orifice outward appearance' is basically our town motto," proclaimed the mayor, to whom they had not been properly introduced, "but that is not official at this point. Soon, though, I hope. Most likely this time next week we will have enough committee votes."

Kearth, who apparently wasn't paying much attention, bluntly asked the mayor of Smelton how they could live in a town that smelled so bad on the outskirts but was almost fragrant on the inside. The mayor said, "?" (Her bodily expression took on a shrugging-shoulders manner while the smile continued to play across her entire being.)

"It works for us, and we don't understand exactly how it happens," she said. "It appears, according to those in our friendly—did I mention how friendly we all are?—town who know best about such things that we just happen to be in this convenient little area between these two mountains, there and over there." The mayor pointed there and over there for effect. "The way the wind comes through the two mountains, which we are so grateful for by the way—well, it brings fresh air into our town and pushes the, you know . . . smell . . . away. Even better than that, at certain times of the year when there are flowers on the sides of the mountains or in the small hill that's behind us, the wind joyousfully—that's my word of course—brings that, that smell, that fragrant smell, into our awaiting town, and it just smells so nice and I'm actually very happy to live here and even happier to be the mayor. I don't think I did, but did I mention that my name is Mayor Maggie?"

Fhfyrd replied, missing the fact that they had just been officially, although single-sidedly, introduced, "So you have a natural protection on the outside because you're surrounded mostly by mountains, but in front you have a barrier of terrible odor so that anyone or anything approaching feels lightheaded and may collapse. That means armies trying to attack or bandits trying to steal from you are thwarted and your townsfolk are safe and sound. Pure genius."

"I'm not actually sure if they are thwarted," said Mayor Maggie, "because I'm not sure I know what the word *thwarted* means. But it intrigues me, and so I would agree just based on the pleasant and confident sound of the word."

"Well, this is completely amazing," Rol said, "and I don't know how we happened upon your friendly town, but I think I can speak for my companions here as well as myself that we would like to stay a little while, if we could do so without putting anyone out."

"With absolute certainty," said the mayor, heartily slapping Rol and Kearth on their backs at the same time, "and I don't even need to get committee approval on that one. It would be entirely our pleasure to have you stay here as long as you wish. We can clean up your clothes and possibly find your horses—I heard they ran off—and we welcome you to stay in any one of our houses. You look like brave warriors that have traveled far, and we would love to hear your stories. As you might imagine, we don't get many visitors here, so any outsiders—friendly outsiders, that is—are welcome. Any nonfriendly outsiders are not as welcome but are nonetheless curiosities around here. There is actually going to be a banquet tonight, and all townsfolk, although not required, are mandated to attend. A fine point, but it was a committee decision to use that wording. Tonight we celebrate Smelton's anniversary and would love to have you as honored guests. Even though you are just arriving. We're friendly. Did I mention that already?"

The banquet was beyond their imagination.

It was a sit-down affair, outdoors in the town center, and everyone was in their best clothes, including Rol, Kearth, and Fhfyrd, though none of them owned much and so had little choice over their choice of clothes. Family members sat together, unless someone or other was on the town committee, in which case the whole family group sat with Mayor Maggie and the guests of honor. Apparently, everyone brought their own chairs, as there were seats of all shapes and sizes lining the long tables that had been made specifically for the occasion. The townsfolk talked in considerate whispers as they waited to be served.

The food was served in a completely fair and just manner, with each person having an opportunity to take food to others, as determined by the course. The first course—breads of all kinds, rolls of many shapes and sizes, beanbutter and cream as toppings, and a strange yellow-green leafy plant as a side—was brought out by youngers of all ages.

Laughter erupted when a bowl toppled to the ground, whether by accident or because of a challenge to determine who could carry the most, but it was cleaned up quickly with no harm done. A very young male younger decided that rolls should be delivered by actually rolling them in the dirt, and it became a teaching moment about the proper way to serve food, with many side conversations and stories of other legendary food mishaps by fathers and mothers alike.

Drinks were brought out by the older youngers, as they could best determine who could receive the ale and who should receive the honeyjuice instead. Even though there were plenty of underage youngers who joked about being old enough to partake in imbibing the ale, when a mug of the delightful, seasonal honeyjuice was placed in front of them, they drank it quietly, enjoying every last drop while breathing into their mugs, making a playful cacophony of whispered echoes. Rol and his companions were, of course, given honeyjuice, and they were happy with that, as they had been drinking water for most of their travels. Kearth drank his juice rapidly, and when he finished, he asked for another mugful, please and thank you.

Those around him all synchronously tilted their heads and looked at him as though they had never heard someone ask for seconds. Kearth, slightly embarrassed and mostly confused, decided not to ask the question again and wished he had not finished his drink so quickly. As a friendly gesture, Rol poured some of his yet untasted juice into Kearth's mug and nodded with a smile. Ale was poured into the mugs of those old enough to drink it, and many hands were gently slapped as husbands, or wives, or both, reached for the drink before the official toast celebrating the occasion was given by Mayor Maggie. When all drinks were in front of the guests, the mayor raised her mug, invited all present to do the same, and repeated the town's anniversary toast: "May we all smell more, stink less, and . . ."

At that very moment, everyone cheered interruptingly, including Fhfyrd, Rol, and Kearth, who were perplexed but felt that they should go along with the apparent ritual. Drinks were drunk, mugs were brought down on the table rapidly and forcefully, and everyone readied themselves for the second course, of course.

The second course was delivered by young elders, married and unmarried alike. Meats of all types, odors, and levels of doneness from raw to crisply burnt. Mounds of substances unknown to Rol but colorful and fragrant enough to at least try. Vegetables of various shapes and cooked or uncooked supposedly to perfection, as the comments confirmed.

While everyone was eating, Rol asked about the anniversary and the toast.

The mayor replied proudly, "This is our town's thirty-eighth anniversary. We celebrate every five years, and have continued that tradition since the beginning. It is important for each of us to participate, as we all have a role in the success of our town."

Having done the math in his head, Rol was just about to ask about the off-timing of the anniversary celebration and inquire about the interestingly unfinished toast when the third and final course came. Dessert.

It came by way of the eldest elders, those most respected of townsfolk.

The sight of the colorful and never-ending desserts brought tears to Kearth's eyes. Large bowls of aromatic mush were placed on each table, which he recognized as berrysmash, one of his favorites from childhood. Plates of cakes drizzled with honey and chivedrip. Offerings of roasted frostbark topped with hazelcream. Fruit-flavored breads and slices of unidentifiable pies were set before the guests, as were containers of after-dinner fruit drinks of every kind. There was everything a weary and amazingly still-hungry traveler could ask for, and more.

And more.

Someone even made *stinky* buns as a joke, but they were not well received and remained untouched. Kearth tried small portions of each good dessert twice, just to make sure he would ultimately make the best decision. Then, instead of asking for more, he just grabbed two full servings of what he wanted, an approach that had the full approval of the hosts. It was a feasting dream come true, and the trio topped off the meal with reckless abandon. When finished, the guests and townsfolk—children and all—sat back in their chairs without a word, without a movement. Rol tried not to fidget.

The mayor asked Kearth if he would like to stand and end the meal with a prayer of thanksgiving. Kearth looked at Rol and Fhfyrd. He stood up. Then he sat down. He leaned close to Rol and said through tight lips, "Do you think you could do it instead?" He settled back in his chair and pointed to his throat, as though something was caught in it, preventing him from speaking.

Rol stood up, and all present bowed their heads. Rol prayed aloud from his heart, and it was the perfect end to the celebration.

CHAPTER 23

BREAKFAST IS INCLUDED

After the banquet, Rol and his companions had time to wander around the town by themselves. With no townsfolk nearby, they felt they could talk freely.

"This is just weird," Fhfyrd mentioned, almost under his breath. "This is too good to be true."

Rol said that it was maybe not too good to be true but maybe just true. Fhfyrd added, in his protective manner of speaking, "I would hate to be caught off guard by staying here and falling under their, dare I say, spell."

"You mean *smell*?" quipped Kearth.

Chuckling at that quick comeback, Rol replied, "I don't think we have to worry about that, but we should be on guard nonetheless. In the meantime, let's find ourselves someplace to stay and be comfortable for at least one night."

As they were still talking about the town and wondering how long they should stay and where they should go next, the mayor approached them to discuss sleeping arrangements. Each of them was to stay in a different residence. There was no room for all of them to stay, at least not comfortably, in one location, so they would have to split up. Fhfyrd was not at all happy about that plan because he felt that splitting up invited the possibility of danger. He pulled Roll and Kearth aside to discuss the matter further. Rol finally convinced them all, even himself, that they probably had nothing to fear, although, again, they needed to be cautious and not get caught off guard.

Escorted by Mayor Maggie, they went to their temporary homes, where townsfolk took them in, and truth be told, they found the accommodations extremely welcoming and more than comfortable. And that was not just because they had been traveling for so long and sleeping under many different and inhospitable conditions. The host families were abundantly gracious.

In the morning, the travelers woke up, and according to their agreement the night before, they met in the town square, or parallelogram, actually—noted by Rol—to determine what to do next.

Rol had been thinking. He decided it would be a good idea for them to stay at least one more night. Probably, though, just the one night. It seemed the right thing to do, and Rol believed that his companions and he needed some much-deserved rest, decent food, and comforting surroundings. And the company of the townsfolk couldn't hurt. Rol secretly rather liked telling stories of their adventure so far to a new audience, and he thought that he might as well take advantage of the opportunity. According to the map, it appeared that they still had a long journey ahead, and so he was thinking that down the road, literally, they would look back and cherish the time they had spent in the town of Smelton.

Fhfyrd was cautious. But truthfully, he was looking forward to the extended stay since he had a hunch that they would be traveling in harsh conditions soon enough. So he agreed that they should stay one more night, and all three travelers were content with that decision.

While they were discussing the matter, the mayor—looking bright and as fresh as ever in the morning sun—greeted them in the town square and thanked them for staying in Smelton. She had heard from some of the locals the stories the journeyers had told, and late into the night in at least one case. Apparently, the townsfolk were excited about the visitors and all were abuzz with talk. Rol blushed, followed by Kearth and then Fhfyrd, as they had all been up late, fascinating the host families with witty recountings of their daring adventures.

Mayor Maggie said that they were welcome to stay as long as they wanted, and if they decided to remain for an extended period of time, she could find them work to do so that they felt useful around town and a part the community. Rol spoke up and said that while they were happy to stay the prior night and were discussing the possibility of one more night, he felt that they should be on their journey no later than the next day. The mayor expressed her happiness with handshakes all around and said, "Maybe you'll change your mind, but either way, we are happy to have you as guests for this brief though rewarding time." She shook hands with each of them again.

The breakfast they shared was even more beyond their imagination than the previous night's banquet.

While they were in the town, Rol and his companions sought out supplies that they might need for the continuing journey. Kearth found a wooden wagon that he thought would come in handy. It was made to be pulled by a lone person, and he had never seen anything like it. The wagon had large wheels that could move easily over most terrain, which Kearth thought was a fantastic idea. Fhfyrd agreed, without any wisecracks. It had a platform with little wooden walls on the sides, so that anything put into it—as long as it wasn't too large—would be contained inside the space.

The wagon was not large, but it was big enough to carry at least the three packs' worth of supplies that they had been lugging around for many days. Two poles sticking out the front of the device made it possible for a person to pull it, with the wagon trailing behind in much the way a cart trails behind a horse, but just barely like that.

Kearth tried it out and cleverly noticed, upon hearing it from the empathetic wagon salesman, that the way it was constructed made it possible for the person to pull a large amount of equipment without adversely affecting the person's back, as the weight was distributed in a better manner than with a single pack. Kearth was vulnerable when the insightful salesman mentioned that with the wagon, someone could carry three packs instead of just one, and that thought kept rolling around in Kearth's mind. He imagined one person—not him, because he would be the proud owner of the contraption—pulling all three packs while the other two travelers rested. Kearth imagined adding to the functionality with some kind of strapping tied around the person to help him pull the wagon more easily. The salesman mentioned a reasonable price and offered to throw in a small container of bright blue coloring for free, in case Kearth decided to add some racing stripes. He offered a second container provided that Kearth made the purchase in the next few moments, which basically sealed the deal.

There was another consideration in the mix as Kearth contemplated the wagon. Earlier that morning the mayor announced that the townsfolk had searched for the missing horses, but they were not to be found. Mayor Maggie would have gladly offered horses to replace them, but there were no horses in the town of Smelton.

Kearth was beside himself with excitement. As they continued on their long journey, the wagon would make it possible for him, or preferably someone else, to transport equipment with ease. Admittedly, the load couldn't be as much as a horse could pull—and definitely not as much as two horses could pull in a full-size wagon—but this human-size wagon would work perfectly for their needs. To top it all off, there was the low, low price of a single gold coin—for one day only! It was definitely Kearth's lucky day, and he could not pass up the once-in-a-lifetime opportunity. He purchased the wagon for the coming journey with one of his last gold coins.

The next day, Rol, Fhfyrd, Kearth, and Kearth's wagon said good-bye to Smelton. And with each of them waving one hand while using the other and a cloth to cover his own nose and mouth, the travelers departed the town. Friendly Mayor Maggie was at the edge of town to see the visitors off and she became smaller and smaller as the visitors continued their journey.

For a while, the traveling trio—especially Kearth—talked about Smelton and the people there, who had been so welcoming and friendly. Although the travelers had been suspicious of the townsfolk at times, their worries were unfounded. The people were just nice, no strings attached, which sounded like a catchy phrase, and Rol made a note of it. The time they had spent in the friendly town seemed to have a positive effect on Kearth, which made Rol smile when he thought about it.

All the trio's belongings had been loaded into Kearth's WonderWagon. For the next two days, they walked, taking a rest every so often during the day, with a longer stop at night. Surprisingly, Kearth volunteered to pull his new purchase the entire time. He did so with a wide grin, downplaying any need for horses, and thinking to himself that soon he would trick one of the others to take over. But for the moment it was actually fun to pull, especially knowing that he was the proud owner of such a clever product.

Eventually, though, they reached rough and extremely rocky terrain where Kearth could not pull the wagon. With great sadness, after having tried heroically to pull the wagon over stones and ruts—even without any packs inside—Kearth realized that he had to leave it behind. Before abandoning it, he patted his great purchase with a loving touch and then kicked one wheel in anger.

That night, Kearth had a dream. In it, the wagon salesman, knowing the route they were traveling, followed them for two days, until the wagon had to be left behind because of the rocky terrain. He waited until the travelers were well out of sight, and then he hitched himself up to the wagon and headed back to town. But not before admiring the blue racing stripes Kearth had added. "Nice touch," said the salesman. He stopped a few times along the way to load the wagon with wild sunfruit, and he was ready to sell the fruit and upgraded wagon to the next gullible customer when he made it back to Smelton.

Kearth woke the next morning whining more than he usually did, at least in terms of the frequency of his whining before Smelton. Days later, he was still complaining about having spent the precious gold coin on that piece of junk, and how ridiculous and unreasonable it was. He never returned to see if the wagon remained where he had left it, blue stripes and all, and that unknown stayed with him the rest of his life.

One morning soon after the wagon debacle, Kearth woke up earlier than Rol and Fhfyrd. He stood up right away, stretching and shaking off the morning dew. Those actions were much different from the way he started most days. As his two companions were stirring, but had not yet risen from the semi-damp ground, Kearth said, "I feel good about today. Yes, good."

Rol replied sleepily, "Feeling sanguine, are we?"

Kearth scratched the back of his neck for no reason, other than an instinctive feeling that he should be scratching. "Sanguine? No, I don't think so. Doesn't that mean melancholy, depressed, or even downhearted? That's certainly not me. Not today."

"No, in fact, sanguine is actually none of those. I think it has a bad reputation for being those, probably because of the way the word sounds. It actually means cheerful or hopeful—optimistic even." If dictionaries had been invented back then, Rol would have been considered a walking one.

"That's me, then. Yes. Sanguine." Kearth tried the word on for size, and it fit well.

"Good," Rol encouraged him. "Then that will be your word for the day. You have to work it smoothly into at least three separate conversations before going to sleep."

"I accept your challenge," countered Kearth, and he smiled broadly for the first time since the must-leave-the-Wonder-Wagon-behind episode.

As it turned out, there was not much conversation that day. Kearth used the word once in the morning when he mentioned how sanguine he was about using the word *sanguine* in at least three conversations, but Rol and Fhfyrd agreed that his use didn't count. Still hopeful, Kearth considered using it on a couple of other occasions but couldn't quite work the word in. By late in the day, he had forgotten all about the challenge, and the word was not mentioned again until two days later. That's when Rol described a colorful grove of trees using the words *sanguine*, *ecru*, and *umber*, much to Kearth's dismay and confusion, since he did not know *sanguine* had multiple meanings.

The word was not used throughout the rest of the journey. Rol, Kearth, and Fhfyrd each—separately and without informing the other two—made a mental note that Sanguine would be a nice name for a daughter, if the occasion ever presented itself, and if the future wife agreed, of course.

As a follow-up, to Kearth's credit and perseverance, although *sanguine* was not spoken again, he managed to work the following words into conversations during the journey: *portent*, *antiphrastic*, *lugubrious*, and *tchotchke*, although the latter took some doing.

CHAPTER 24

EPIC SALAD

Soon after—as journeys go that means four to five days later, after some activity that is not important enough to mention—Rol said, "Don't all great adventures have some kind of song or ballad about them? For posterity or other such things?"

Kearth and Fhfyrd looked at him and shrugged. "We guess so," came the response from both of them, although it was really a combination of "I guess so," said by each.

"What we need—us, right now—is an adventure song or ballad . . . a Salad. About our adventures so far," Rol added excitedly as they continued walking.

"Any time you want to start is fine with me," lazily retorted Kearth. His previous good mood, the subsequent bad mood, and then the good mood of the past few days had worn off.

"OK, then, I'll start," said Rol. "What if we began singing a few words and then it would turn into a Salad?"

"Why don't you go ahead and start, instead of talking about starting?" Kearth said less lazily and more wearily.

"Well, OK," started Rol. "OK . . . So I can't think of anything at all. Does anyone else want to go first?"

"We can't think of anything, either," came the response, again from both of them, although it was really a combination of "I can't think of anything, either," said by Kearth, and "I don't care," by Fhfyrd.

Rol started again. "What if we start with mentioning 'Walking on a long journey' and then 'We were on our feet all day, every day'—that's good. Then we get to 'Carrying heavy loads through the continuous rain and wind'—but it really hasn't rained every day. How about 'Carrying heavy loads through the glaring sun beating down on us and our extremely heavy loads'? Sounds good, keep going. Then 'We have walking sticks and snakes on the ground and we have to watch out for the snakes and we poke them with our sticks'—that's exciting, but that never happened. This is more difficult than I thought."

"Do you think everything has to fit into your Salad? Even things that didn't happen to us, like snakes on the ground?" questioned Kearth alone, as apparently this was a conversation not involving Fhfyrd. He didn't seem to care.

Or he was working on his own Salad in his own secretly nonaloof mind, planning to play it on his lyre.

"The Salad doesn't have to cover everything we have done, or even things that we haven't done, but I'm trying to make it more exciting," answered Rol.

"By adding sticks and snakes? They don't even rhyme," retorted Kearth.

"It can rhyme if you help me think of something that rhymes with sticks."

"I can't think of anything."

"What rhymes with snakes, then?"

"Let me think. Here we go, got it. Are you ready? 'Every step the trio takes they have to watch the ground for snakes.'"

"Let's go back to sticks."

"You don't approve of my rhyme?"

"It's just . . . It's just not true, like you said. And it's also not Salad material. Let's skip the sticks and snakes and come up with something more epic, and more true to what we have done. That should make the words come more easily. They'll come from memory and not imagination."

"So we're moving away from snakes? What if we encounter snakes along the way, later at some point?"

"Then we could possibly add them back in."

"And use my line?"

"Possibly."

"What did we say about rain, then? Lots of words rhyme with rain."

"We didn't come to a conclusion about rain, but I was not necessarily adding rain since it isn't raining now, and that makes it hard to get in the rainy, dreary, epic mood worthy of a Salad."

"But nobody will know that it isn't raining today, will they? I say we add rain and make it work, since we can rhyme with that. Plus, it's a retelling of an adventure and there needs to be a few challenges."

"Other than snakes."

"Other than snakes, yes."

"Good. I think we're finally getting somewhere," said Rol.

"What if we mention not having enough to eat? That's true enough, and I'm thinking about that right now," said Kearth.

"You mean talking about how someone forgot to buy enough food for the three of us in the last town, which I think is rude?" The words were finally coming from Fhfyrd.

"Yes, er, no. Not exactly what I meant. But nice rhyme," said Kearth.

"It rained a lot and wet is what they got," clumsily sing-songed Rol.

"There is potential, but you need to brush up on

your meter . . . I mean, what about food? Don't change the subject," griped Fhfyrd.

"Look who is involved in the Salad conversation now. Now that someone is hungry," said Kearth.

"I'm involved because I'm hungry, yes," said Fhfyrd. "And I'm hungry because someone with the initials *K*—and that's it, *K*—forgot to buy food for us when we were in the last town, as we all previously agreed that he would do. So I believe I have every right to be hungry, and cantankerous for that matter, and I would like to know how we are going to get food, and focus on that instead of trying to come up with a sballad or whatever it is . . ."

"Salad," answered Rol.

". . . wasting time on a salad," continued Fhfyrd, "when we should be thinking about what we are going to eat."

"Good stuff," said Kearth in a positive reinforcement manner. "They had no food and were in a bad mood. Epic. Drama and action. Legendary. And it rhymes. What do you think, Rol?"

Rol was distracted by a whisper in his ear. As he looked at his companions still discussing the finer points of creating an epic Salad, he realized the whisper did not come from them. Almost immediately, he heard a noise in the brush behind him, as though something fell or was thrown there, landing heavily. Then he heard shuffling coming from the other direction. When he looked that way, he thought he saw movement, but he couldn't be sure because of the dim light at that time of day and the small trees swaying nearby in the wind.

Fhfyrd and Kearth stopped talking and watched Rol, with perplexed expressions to match his.

Slowly and carefully, Rol walked over to the noise in the brush. He saw a strange, colorful stick poking out. It was odd because he had just walked by that area with his friends and did not notice it. Upon closer review—pulling the stick out of the ground—he realized it was not just an interesting growth from a bush. It was actually a spear that presumably had been thrown at him but missed him and landed in a bush, hence the whisper in his ear and the thud on the ground. All that was obvious now.

Then he realized—almost before it was too late—that another nicely colored spear was headed right for him. He ducked just in time for the sharp, flying weapon to lodge itself in a nearby tree instead of in him.

Suddenly, he noticed that even though he was crouched down, he was higher than his companions, who had stopped debating and were flat on the ground, looking around nervously.

It didn't take Rol long to also fall to the ground, his face pressed down and his belongings gathered around, covering him as much as possible so that he would not be seen, which was a good thought but not entirely realistic. Realizing the dire nature of the situation, with the three of them being out in the open and needing to find cover or run, Rol tried to focus on their best options, though none were coming to mind. Determined to be proactive, he resisted the urge to fidget in the tense situation and was surprisingly successful.

An unexpected smile appeared on Kearth's face. "Quick!" he whispered semi-loudly.

"You have a plan?" whispered Rol, matching Kearth's quiet but not quiet enough volume.

"*Quick* rhymes with *stick*," said Kearth proudly and inappropriately in the dire situation. Had he been standing instead of splayed on the ground, about to be speared, he would have attempted to pat himself on the back.

Fresh noises coming from the direction where the spears had probably originated prompted the three to peer into the semi-darkness. They saw movement but no identifiable shapes, which appeared to be a number of beings or creatures, though they could not make out what they were.

At that moment, in the near dark, they realized that they were most likely outnumbered, in a foreign land, uncomfortably hungry, with rain starting, and their Salad was going nowhere.

The three braced for an attack and then heard, "Sorry. Thought yuns were someone not you. Have gooder nights."

And the Eye Lender . . . er, *Highlander* tribe scurried by, helping the trio to their feet but continuing on, apparently on a mission.

Kearth mumbled to himself almost incessantly on the heels of encountering the tribe again, and after a couple of days of monotonous trekking, he announced confidently, "I think I have it. Yes. A Salad to top all Salads."

Rol and Fhfyrd were startled out of their trek-trances and stopped abruptly. They looked at Kearth, then at each other, then back at Kearth. In their semi-stupor, Rol and Fhfyrd swiftly sat down on the all-too-dusty ground in unison, leaned back on their packs, and listened.

"Ahem," started Kearth, in the midst of the rising dust cloud, trying to clear it from his throat so that he could present his verbal work of art properly.

"Here goes . . ."

"Three they were, and thus they journeyed
Over mountain, under sky.
Ne'erending danger pressed
From front and back and every side.
Beings strange and creatures stranger,
Found in towns and swamps and holes.
Treading forward, ever onward,
Traveled three undaunted souls.

Ceaseless rain and biting cold,
Raging storms and quenchless thirst.
Never giving in or hopeless,
Knowing life is blessed, not cursed.
Story's ending in their grasp,
Soon to find where answer lies.
What remains?—A few more steps and
Wiping tears of joy from eyes."

"I didn't think you had it in you. It's just right," complimented Fhfyrd.

"I agree. I bet Fhfyrd could put a nice tune to it," also complimented Rol.

They were in a good yet also melancholic mood for the rest of the day. It had been quite an odyssey, and they still had a long way to go, but they would go with more of a spring in their step. At least for the time being.

CHAPTER 25

DAISIES AND OTHER DISTRACTIONS

"I had a rabbit once," mentioned Kearth.

"You had a rabbit?" replied Fhfyrd.

"Yes, but I don't have him any longer."

"This sounds uncomfortably familiar. Of course you don't have him."

"No, really, I had a rabbit, and his name was Fluff. He was all white, and he didn't like me."

"He didn't like you? Was it something you tried to feed him?"

"No, of course not. I fed him fresh carrots from the garden and daily brushed his hair with a soft pineytree branch."

"You brushed his hare, that's good. I get it."

"I'm not kidding—he was a good pet. But then he had to go."

"He had to go? He was a rabbit. Why or where did he have to go?"

"It was a relationship thing. He didn't like me and he bit me."

"So you had to let him go. I see."

"No, he just left. On his own one day."

"Wait, why did he bite you?"

"Looking back, now I believe it was because I called him names."

"Why did you call him names?"

"Because he wouldn't listen to me."

"So you called him names? What kind of names did you call this rabbit?"

"Obviously, names that rabbits don't like to be called."

"So he left you."

"He did. And it was sudden. I realize now that I should not have called him names. Or I would still have him right now."

"Yes, quite. So at least you learned something."

"Absolutely, I learned something. Now I see how important that is. No more name-calling. It's wrong, and I apologize for calling either of you any names, other than your given names, of course."

Rol and Fhfyrd shrugged at each other, as they wondered what names Kearth had been calling them.

"I will not say words of anger any longer. This is the new me," promised the new Kearth, standing a little straighter, as they walked into the sunrise.

"When will this accursed path ever end?" barked Kearth later that afternoon. And for good measure, he spat on the ground. "I grow weary of this sameness." He spat again. Kearth had started spitting a few days prior and gradually increased doing so, depending on the situation. He spat to accent every statement he made about his discomfort. If he were happy, he wouldn't spit. If he was mad, he might. If tired, he probably would yawn, with the spitting drool coming out of his open mouth in a passive manner, though it could still be considered spit material. If he was excited, he might double-spit or do nothing at all. Generally, though, when he didn't spit it was on purpose, with him holding on for the moment that it could be used for the greatest effect.

Fhfyrd and Rol reminded Kearth often about his anger promise, but for the time being, he spat. Throwing all spitting caution to the wind, as it were, even though there was no wind at that time.

The path stretched on in front of them, not wavering for a moment, even though it got spat upon repeatedly and annoyingly.

The three travelers walked through the day. Their progress on the last half-day was more like semi-controlled stumbling, but they eventually came to something that wasn't a path—it was a stream. Technically, a stream can be a path to someone or something, so it is not entirely pathless in nature, but to Fhfyrd, Kearth, and Rol, it was a change of scenery and a temporary respite from path-sameness.

They stopped to investigate. And to look for creatures beneath rocks, of course.

Stream creatures were not to be found, and the threat of more sameness loomed. They knew they would have to continue walking, but they could not do that until they had their fill of something different.

Then it happened.

Something entirely different from the path, or even the stream. Unfortunately, it was not the kind of different they were hoping for. This different was painful. Almost as painful as it was completely unexpected.

They were ambushed. Utterly caught off guard in their boredom.

In fact, the attack was so sudden and unexpected that, for just a few moments, all three of them welcomed it, at first smiling and then shaking their heads in disbelief. It was pain that soon brought them back to their senses. The stabbing pain of a thousand spears penetrating the top layer of skin and then going further, into nerves they did not realize they had. Which is not surprising, since nerves were not a topic of discussion among semi-civilized persons in this generally unenlightened age.

As luck—for those who believe in such a thing—would have it, the thousand spearettes were launched by an army of tiny creatures, most with such horrible aim as to completely miss something that was, relative to themselves, the size of a significant mountain. But with the attackers severely outnumbering their targets—in this case, approximately ten thousand to three—good aim was not considered exactly critical.

Rol brushed the spearettes from his lower leg. The sound of hundreds of shafts of wood cracking was deafening to the tiny warriors, who fell to the ground with earaches unimaginable.

"Do not retreat, my fellow warriors!" shouted the pint-size herculean warrior leader. "Our foes will be vanquished beneath the heels of our thundering boots."

The spears in Rol's leg caused but a fleeting moment of discomfort. Covering an area smaller than his thumbnail, they were not terribly disconcerting to him.

Kearth, on the other hand—or the lower leg to be exact—received more spear pricks than Rol and Fhfyrd combined, and although his wound covered a patch of skin the size of two thumbnails plus a pinky nail, it was more annoying than bothersome. In his annoyed state, Kearth grabbed a small branch from a nearby tree-tree tree and used it as a switch to swat at the pierced area. Again came the thunderous sound of wooden shafts splintering, as heard by the less-than-ant-sized warriors, who were fearsome when facing opponents their own diminutive size.

"We have them!" cried the itsy-bitsy hero. "Victory shall be ours!"

Kearth spat absentmindedly and wiped out an entire battalion of the tiny but muscular fighters, who did not know whether to launch a second round of spears or flee like wee little baby people. The sound of the remaining seven thousand angry warriors—a sound that would not be heard again for a millennium—wafted in the air but was wasted on the three travelers, who trudged on while noticing nothing more than a light buzzing sound.

"I hope I'm not allergic to bug bites," said Kearth, spitting.

"I said, 'Fresh as a daisy,'" said Fhfyrd upon waking the next morning.

"Enough of your Fhfyrdfoolery. How are we supposed to know what 'Fresh as a daisy' means?" responded Kearth, on the verge of spitting.

"Fresh as a daisy. That's all there is. That's it. It says what it says and there's nothing more. I mean, what else could it mean? And I'm not trying to be condescending."

"There's no reason to be condescending, or even to talk down to me. I don't know what being 'fresh as a daisy' means. I could guess, I guess, but . . . No, I don't think I could even guess. I don't know what it means. There's nothing wrong with me. I just have never heard that choice of words. 'Fresh as a daisy' frankly means absolutely nothing to me. Why should it? It sounds foolish and nonsensical. Why would someone intelligent, or even smart like me, say something is as fresh as a daisy? When I . . ."

"You're taking this too far, you know. It isn't that important. You're making entirely too big of a deal about this," Fhfyrd countered.

Kearth disagreed heartily. "Too big of a deal? What does that mean? Why do you talk in riddles? Are you making up phrases and testing them on me to see how I react in certain circumstances? Am I some kind of experiment? An animal that you are testing your preposterous word thingies on to see if I . . . crack or something? Is that what this is about? Is it? Is it?!"

"No, actually, it was just supposed to be the start of pleasant conversation. Not a trick, not an experiment, although that sounds like fun—and I thank you for the idea, which I will try to use to my advantage at a later date—but, no, it was nothing of the sort. I think it quite odd that you became so worked up about the whole situation, and I think I deserve an apology for your accusatory tone."

"My what?" questioned Kearth, obviously offended and puzzled.

"Would you two knock it off?" reprimanded Rol.

CHAPTER 26

IN THE END, FAMILIAR FACES

It rained for three days straight. At one point the sky appeared to consider *not* raining, but then it decided against it and rained all the harder. Three days and three nights of sopping, uncomfortable wetness.

Yet through it all, Rol whistled joyfully, remembering tunes he had learned from DaTerrin. On the first day, when it started to rain in the morning, Rol began to whistle. Later, after they had their lunch of wet crackers and even wetter stew, Rol continued to whistle, although the crackers played havoc with his whistler for quite some time. On and on he whistled, through the rain, through the rain, through the rain. It was as if he enjoyed the rain. The others were too miserable to question him, and also a little fearful of stopping the sound, which would make the situation most entirely unbearable. Somehow the pleasant chirps, even when off-key, brought a promise of sunshine and hope.

Finally, after three full days, the rain stopped. It was late afternoon, and the sun, peaking through the clouds on its way to setting for the day, was glorious to behold. The three travelers stopped and beheld. Rol's whistling ceased. All noises within hearing range ended. There was no sound, although Fhfyrd would probably have sworn, if he were pressed to do so, that they could hear the sun setting. They could certainly see it. And each of them felt it. Tasting it would have been going too far, but at that moment, when they were beholding one of the most beautiful sights they had ever beheld—especially after the recent unpleasant days they had endured—hearing it was not necessarily out of the question. With the day's last sparkle in their eyes, the sun set onto, and then comfortably into, the horizon.

Even though it was time to settle down for the evening, Rol was beyond excited. With just another few days of walking, he should be home. The hand-drawn map that had led him through the incredible journey was now almost useless, other than as a memento of his travels. He had started his trek alone, but now he pictured walking into his village and greeting his family with his new friends.

The next two days went by quickly. Talk between the

three travelers was a flurry at times, and then there would be silence for long periods as they walked, each lost in thought. All three were excited and ready for the journey to end while also wishing that it would continue.

Waking up on the morning of what was to be the final day of travel, Rol opened his eyes to find that Kearth and Fhfyrd were already awake. They were not bickering or even talking in low voices. They were still, and Rol felt the beautiful peace all around him. His companions were on their knees, with their eyes closed and faces lifted toward the rising sun as they prayed silently.

Rol had no words. His eyes filled with tears, and a quivering smile came to his lips. His heart felt as though it would burst. He walked over and knelt near Kearth and Fhfyrd. The three of them greeted the morning with silent prayers of thanks and joy.

It was a moment that Rol would describe later as the most inspiring and fulfilling of the journey. Something had changed in his two traveling companions. Rol was not sure if the transfiguration would last through the day, or stretch into many days, but at the moment it didn't matter. He was just grateful to experience it.

After a quick morning meal, they were on their way. As the day progressed, Rol started to recognize familiar sights:

an open field where he used to play tag with friends; a winding river where he swam and lifted rocks to find the creatures beneath them; trees he remembered climbing that were just on the fringe of being an acceptable distance from home for a younger of his age, and actually slightly beyond that. Then he saw the buildings of his village in the distance—houses, stores, and gathering places that had not changed in all the time he had been gone. Rol did not have any reason to think that they would be different, even though *he* definitely was.

Close to the village, they heard the sound of a bell ringing five times. As they moved closer still, they were surprised to see no one in the fields, on paths, in their yards, or around their homes. The three travelers walked into the empty village square and heard a voice that Rol recognized immediately.

The word "Welcome!" was followed by a pause and then, "I had something prepared to say, but I cannot find the words at this time. I just . . ." From Rol's left came his father, his arms spread wide to embrace his returning son. It was a hug that had waited for almost four years, and both father and son felt that it should and would never end.

Rol felt a gentle hand on his shoulder, and when he turned his head, he saw that it was his mother. A new hug, and tears from both of them this time. Then came smaller hugs around Rol's waist from his two sisters, and laughs replaced the tears. A few moments of introductions followed—those in Rol's family introduced to Kearth and Fhfyrd, and vice versa.

Rol's youngest sister said, "But we already know him," referring to Fhfyrd.

Rol's mother replied with, "We'll discuss that later."

Rol was confused, but then his mind moved on to something else when he saw a figure limping toward him, and a completely different and overwhelming confusion set in.

His uncle, A. Loysius DaTerrin—master, teacher, friend—approached Rol.

"I would not be surprised if you have questions, my student," said DaTerrin. "I hope that I can answer them to your satisfaction."

Then the rest of the villagers surrounded them, cheering, shaking hands, wiping tears, shouting for joy. Had high-fives or fist bumps been invented, the moment would have been absolutely full of them.

Large tables were set up right there in the village center for Rol and his immediate family as well as his extended family—DaTerrin, Kearth, and Fhfyrd. Fresh food and cold drinks were also provided, to Kearth's delight. The villagers served the group, and then slowly scattered to give them time to discuss what needed to be discussed, as the bell in the village rang out five more times.

"Son, we have missed you so much," Rol's father said. "It is beyond telling, and I hope you always know that we are grateful for you coming back to us, after what you may have perceived as your mother and I abandoning you. That was not our intention at all. We just needed you to . . . We were counting on you to make the journey to us . . . You are our hope, and now we have you back."

Rol questioned the words "our hope," saying that he did not understand.

Slowly and purposefully, Rol's father began to tell of the plan they had made for Rol to be trained by DaTerrin. There would be as much learning and experience as possible in that setting with his uncle. Then, so that he would understand the world in which they all lived, Rol would embark on a journey.

He would have to make the decisions necessary to survive on his journey, and bring those experiences back as tools and examples for the new role he would assume in the community. Only by making the journey could he obtain the practical wisdom, understanding, right judgment, courage, and knowledge—as well as the awe and respect for God—he would need to lead his people in this world.

Only then could Rol, the student of life, truly *Be*.

His father's words prompted Rol to ask other questions. "Why all this fuss for one person? We have less than two hundred here, in our little valley. All of this, for the past four years, was to prepare me to be a leader of this small village?"

And then he saw them.

People coming over the hills, from towns, villages, hamlets all around. Crossing the bridges into the village, over the rocks, through the fields, and down the paths. Many others, and many more from the communities around them.

They came.

They came to be led by him.

EPILOGUE

Later that day, after the festivities, greetings, and a once-in-a-lifetime-so-far celebration, DaTerrin explained further, "Fhfyrd is actually your older second cousin on your father's side. And his name is really Clem. Not sure where the 'of the Black Mountains' came from, but I enjoy the new name he claimed for himself, clever lad. You met him many, many years ago, but we hoped that you were too young at that time to remember him at this time.

"Apparently, we were correct in making that assumption. After your journey started the way it did, we had second thoughts about you being completely alone and felt it was necessary, and compassionate, to have someone act as a guardian for you. He was instructed not to get in your way but to provide support as you needed. That is why your sister said that she already had met him. We sent for him not long after I arrived here, and then he proceeded to travel quickly to try and meet up with you somewhere along your journey. He took an easier route than you did, although I'm sure he has stories of his own. The black attire was all his idea as well as the supposedly tough demeanor. I don't have any idea what Kearth's story is, but in my experience so far with him, I'm sure I will hear all about it. Anyway, you are here now, and I believe the right decision was made."

"But you . . . I thought it was my fault that you . . ." started Rol, still confused.

"This may be difficult for me to explain and for you to understand," said DaTerrin, "but you deserve answers, and I will do what I can to provide them. I am so very sorry if you felt you were the cause of my disappearance, or even worse, my death. The day on the hill-mountain was so important for you to experience—God's nature-blessings in all their wonder. We stayed late because it was difficult for you to leave without seeing the sunset, and that was understandable. None of that was your fault.

"I actually had made plans to leave you on your own in a different way, as arranged with your parents and others in the village. It might take you time to forgive me, or us, and I recognize that. Or possibly it already has happened.

"It was a completely unexpected situation when the grumblegoblins arrived and took me, and I honestly had a difficult time getting away from them, as they can be very persistent in their own uncivilized way. In the end, the result was the same, which was to have you on your own for a period of time—though possibly with others if it worked out that way—to give you the opportunity to grow. You needed more training and real experiences than I could give you, and your parents and I felt a journey for you was the best and possibly the *only* way to give you that opportunity. Again, the decision was one that was not arrived at without much consideration and discussion. And frankly, tears.

"You have been told your entire life that there is something different about you. And there is. You are compassionate, positive, insightful, courageous, and humble—a true leader. Something that all in your village and the surrounding communities need desperately to not only survive but also to thrive in these times. As your father mentioned, you are their hope."

"But what about you?" Rol asked his uncle.

"Not me, young one. I am needed in other ways, in other places."

Rol paused thoughtfully and then said, "I needed you. I was angry and alone. Somehow I did know that you were still alive. Somehow I knew that, inside of me. It was an awful time for me when you were taken away, and even after that. But I forgive you. I understand now.

"The journey I was on . . . it was so much more than just traveling day after day, learning to cope with situations and overcome challenges. I discovered that there are many things that pull you in one direction or another, sometimes asking or forcing you to make difficult decisions. There is also help from many different sources, if you let them help. And you never know what surprises await you, so you need to be prepared for many situations. The journey was life changing, and I don't say that lightly. I had to learn to be who I was meant to be, and now here I am—just one person, but ready to make a difference in a great big world. I'm so grateful to God for the opportunity, and to those who helped me—helped us—along the way.

"After everything that happened, it's just starting to sink in that I'm here with you, my family, and even the two interesting characters I found along the way that have become my good friends. But, believe it or not, through it all, I never gave up hope that I would see you and my family again."

"That's the important part," replied DaTerrin, "You never gave up hope. I knew you had it in you. We all did."

Experiencing the warm reunion of Rol and DaTerrin, Rol and his family, Rol and his village, Fhfyrd and Kearth were overjoyed for their traveling partner of those many months. Despite their joy, they were quiet while reflecting on their part in the adventure, sitting and leaning against a tree on the edge of town. The difficult journey was worth the effort. Not that they would do it all over again . . .

"I guess this is a case of hometown boy makes good, huh?" said Fhfyrd.

"What does that even mean?" questioned Kearth.

"Well, I . . . I don't know exactly. It's just something I heard once. I thought it was appropriate to say on this particular occasion. Anyway, this is a good story. I hope someone was taking notes."

"Er . . . yeah, me too."

Taking out his lyre, Fhfyrd started to tune the strings, preparing to play music to accompany the Salad that Kearth had written many days before—and finally warming up to the idea. Suddenly, the thinnest string pulled loose and then caught a breeze, floating off to its own next adventure.

"Well, I guess that's that, then," said Fhfyrd, shaking his head and smiling.

"Like I've always said, you can never trust a lyre," snickered Kearth as he hurried off to tell Rol the Returned about the latest mishap, and to consider together what had been . . . and what was yet to be.

ACKNOWLEDGEMENTS

This journey required the assistance of many to complete, and I am grateful for all the words of wisdom, every large and small bit of help, and the prayers of numerous family members and friends.

First of all, I want to acknowledge the Holy Spirit, who guided me throughout this adventure, and provided countless opportunities for me to grow in faith, trust, patience, and perseverance.

A heartfelt and sincere thank you to: my beautiful wife of twenty-five years, Betty, who is the love of my life and who was incredibly supportive and full of invaluable ideas throughout this entire process; our daughter, Lauren, who added so much to this story through her unmatched insight and humor; and our son, Andrew, who provides so much inspiration and for whom this story was written. Thank you also to my parents, Jim and Gail, who have always been there for me no matter what, and who are examples of great hope and perseverance; and my mother-in-law, Betty, who graces our home with her presence every day.

In addition to those listed above, each of whom read the manuscript at one stage or another and provided valuable feedback, many others contributed immensely through suggestions, editing, proofing, and support. My sincerest appreciation goes out to: my lifelong friends, who also happen to be my sisters, Terri Randall and Jen Crider; editorial expert extraordinaire, Robin Cruise; middle-school teacher, Lori Raden, with her gift of encouragement; and an assembly of helpful others who offered advice or humored me by reading the manuscript: Julie Boatright, Bonnie Briceno, Phillipe Desamours, Diane Doyle, Geraldine Erikson, Amy Fries, Peggy Grogan, Margi Loesel, the Marsh family, the Miller family, Father Francis Peffley, the Pugh family, Barb and Kevin Rowe, the Slocumb family, Stephanie Stahl, Father Thomas Vander Woude, Patricia Welch, Jack Wood, and Father Thomas Yehl.

Also at this time I have in mind a friend, Steve Bush, who shared many childhood adventures with me and who recently started on an unexpected journey to reunite with his Heavenly Father.

My prayers and thanks go out to each and every reader of this book—whether a younger or an elder. Enjoy the journey and may God bless you!

Be thankful. Be good. Be who you are meant to be.

Made in the USA
Middletown, DE
26 November 2015